A CLUELESS WOMAN

~~~

A novel by **T. B. MARKINSON**

Published by T. B. Markinson

Visit T. B. Markinson's official website at tbmarkinson.wordpress.com for the latest news, book details, and other information.

Copyright © T. B. Markinson, 2015

Cover Design by Erin Dameron-Hill / EDHGraphics

Edited by Karin Cox and Jeri Walker

Proofread by Kelly Hashway

This book is copyrighted and licensed for your personal enjoyment only. All rights reserved. No part of this publication may be reproduced, stored in a retrieval system, or transmitted in any forms or by any means without the prior permission of the copyright owner. The moral rights of the author have been asserted.

This book is a work of fiction. Names, characters, businesses, places, events, and incidents are the product of the author's imagination or are used fictitiously. Any resemblance to actual persons, living or dead, events, or locales is entirely coincidental.

Chapter One

"I FEEL LIKE A LADY of the night." Meg crammed the wad of twenties I'd just furtively handed over into the pocket of her jeans. "Of course, if things don't turn around for me soon, that might be my future calling. Do ya think William would pay to sleep with me? He was never shy about his desires."

I assumed she'd added that juicy detail about my colleague to bait me. No, to remind me of what she was capable of and to keep me in line. Years of falling for her self-pity and emotional blackmail had taught me to steel myself and ignore Meg to the best of my ability, but I still found myself saying, "I can't keep handing over wads of money."

"Why? We both know you aren't even close to draining your trust fund, not even a quarter of it." Meg leveled her deep-green gaze on my face.

"I'm not responsible for you."

"Responsible for me?" She laughed, bitterly. "Have you been attending Al-Anon meetings or something?"

I sighed. "I need to go." I hoisted my book bag over my shoulder. Meg feigned lunging at me, and I jumped back. We were in an alley behind a coffee shop, and Meg was blocking the street exit. The door to the coffee shop didn't have a handle, and

I assumed it could only be opened from the inside. I moved back, against the wall, inching closer to safety.

"Must be nice to have the luxury of being a student." Her abrasive smile alerted me to tread carefully. My mind flooded with memories of invoking Meg's wrath. She crossed her arms, revealing she had no intention of budging. "How are William and Janice? It's been a long time since I was welcome to join the weekly study sessions." Her eyes lit up. "Hey, I know. I bet William would pay big bucks for me to tell him all about us." She ran a finger down my face, and I willed myself not to cringe. "The things you used to do to me and what you begged me to do to you." She reached for my belt buckle, but I backpedaled, much to her delight. "I bet that'd get him off." She squared her shoulders. "Or you could just meet me next week." Meg patted the wad in her pocket.

"Fine."

A car horn blared, and Meg spun to view the commotion, allowing me to sidle past. Once out of harm's way, on the sidewalk, I turned. "Keep going to your meetings, okay?" I said.

Meg's eyes softened but then quickly coalesced into anger. "Get off your high horse, Lizzie. You aren't perfect. And don't forget" — she stabbed a finger in the air — "next week."

Any retort would just egg her on, so I wheeled around and marched toward the shop's entrance.

"Lizzie!" a shout came from behind me. It wasn't Meg's voice, so I turned.

Janice strode up next to me, hooking her arm through mine. "I thought that was you. Why in the world are you hanging out in a back alley with Meg, of all people?"

"Were you the one who honked?"

She nodded. "I was looking for a parking space and considered the alley when I spied you two. Not sure what got into me. Shock, probably. Or fear."

"Whatever the reason, thanks."

"How much this time?" Her arm tightened on mine.

"Too much."

"You know, you aren't responsible for her."

"So people keep telling me. But it's — "

"Hard. I know. I get it. Meg and I had been best friends before she spiraled out of control. I can't imagine how hard it is for you, being her ex. Besides, she does it to me too." Janice tugged my arm and motioned to a bench outside the trendy coffee shop. "Sit for a moment."

I complied.

"Do you remember the three of us before everything? We were The Three Musketeers. The only girls out of ten students studying under Dr. Marcel." Janice unraveled a chunky knit scarf with a fringe, letting it drape over her shoulders like a shawl.

I laughed. "We had to band together to deal with all the machismo bullshit. Mostly from Jared and Trent."

"God, I was relieved when Trent left last year for Harvard. His leer." She shook it off. "And Jared thinking he was God's gift to all women, even with his lazy eye and stutter!"

"I still remember the night when you told Jared he turned you gay." I laughed.

"And he believed me. No offense, Lizzie, but women are way too much work." Janice nudged my arm.

I wholeheartedly agreed.

"I wonder how he's getting along in Arizona," I said in an effort not to dwell on Meg and the alley situation. My eyes feasted on the Rocky Mountain foothills set against a brilliant lapis sky. I'd rather be hiking to the summit, Horsetooth Rock. I longed to feel free.

"Still can't believe Jared scored a teaching gig before finishing his dissertation." Janice slapped her thigh.

"Come on. His dad is president of the university, and his mom is a state senator. Jared will never have to worry about a job — he'll be tenured in record time."

Janice placed a palm on my thigh. "You recovered from …?" She nodded her head toward the alley. Janice knew me all too well, but she played along for a few moments to allow my skittering heartbeat and ragged breathing to regulate.

I nodded. "Yeah, thanks again for saving me. Again."

"Don't thank me." She groaned. "I'm still mad at myself for not seeing the warning signs about Meg's drinking. Shit, the two of us used to go out together and get hammered." Janice covered half her face with the scarf.

"Hey. Stop that." I pulled her hand away from her face. "You can't blame yourself for Meg."

"I know, I know …" She looked away. I knew all too well the guilt swimming inside her head.

I stood. "We should get inside." She reluctantly followed, and I opened the door and motioned for her to walk ahead. Janice marched to the counter and ordered a beer. It was barely five o'clock, and I playfully rolled my eyes at her.

"Don't start. It's been one hell of a day already." She smiled. Both of us knew today was no different from any other day, and given the conversation we had just ended, it was a tad bit uncomfortable. "You ready for William?" She squeezed my arm.

"I better be. He just walked in." I leaned in and whispered, "Please don't mention you had to rescue me from Meg."

"Like I would." Janice plastered a fake smile on her face and greeted William. "Willy Boy, you ready for tonight's riveting discussion?"

William bristled at the nickname. He was from Rhode Island, and his full name was William Connor Abernathy Thornhill V. He'd actually introduced himself like that when we met at orientation several years ago. I soon learned that none of the Williams in his family went by anything other than William. Janice, though, never quite got that — or never cared much for it.

"Wouldn't miss it for the world," he sneered in his typical way.

With a frosty nod toward me, he ordered himself a beer. I wasn't a teetotaler; however, I wasn't exactly thrilled that we met at a shop that served alcohol after five to drum up business. Not that I never drank, but the three of us met for academic purposes, not social. And when Meg had been a member of the group — well, it made my life harder since she didn't know her limit. I rubbed my eyes to wipe away the memories.

"Shall we sit?" I asked, motioning to our reserved table in the back.

William gestured for Janice to walk ahead of him and said, "Lady first."

She gritted her teeth while I ignored his dig. Since Meg quit the program he went above and beyond to ruffle my feathers. My sole purpose for continuing these sessions was to finish at the top of our PhD program, which meant I couldn't get sucked into William's pettiness.

The three of us met each week at Chippie's Coffee Shop to prepare for our seminars. The name of the venue had never been officially explained, but I assumed it was a play on the chipped cups and pint glasses. Every one I'd been served over the years had been chipped or cracked. Superglue, or what have you, held most of them together, and each week the person with the most damaged cup had the privilege of leading the discussion. William was tonight's winner. It was going to be a long night.

"IT'S OBVIOUS YOU'VE never had mind-blowing sex," William said, and took a massive swig of his second beer. His swarmy smile conveyed that could change if I went to bed with him.

I blinked once. Twice.

Janice just gawped at him and then back at me. Her mouth formed an O, which was unlike her. A spunky San Franciscan, she was normally easy-going and unflappable. Although naturally brilliant, she was a free spirit who didn't give a damn about academia and had entered the history PhD program just to get her parents off her back.

Janice enjoyed the meetings purely as a form of entertainment. As long as she stayed in the program, her parents supported her and left her alone. So far, at least. She hadn't expressed any desire to find a rich guy to marry instead, even though it wouldn't be hard for her to succeed in that endeavor. She reminded me of Audrey Hepburn, just not as skinny. Collin, her on-again-off-again boyfriend since college days, was a decent guy, but Janice was in no rush to settle down, if ever. Whenever he pushed for more, she broke it off. As far as I could tell, her sole ambition was to float through life with no responsibilities or demands.

Seconds later, I was finally able to speak. "And how did you deduce that, exactly?"

"Deduce!" Janice slapped my thigh under the table and chortled. "Lizzie, you crack me up. Go on, Willy Boy." She faced William, who sat opposite of us. "Tell us how you *deduced* that."

From the beginning, he and I had viewed each other as the main competition in the program. His last comment, though, was a step too far and, quite frankly, rude.

"Anyone who says they'd ditch Humphrey Bogart at the end of *Casablanca* obviously hasn't had great sex," he repeated without a trace of humor.

Janice laughed. "Oh, I get it. You're quoting *When Harry Met Sally*."

William and I both pivoted to her, clueless.

"Seriously? Neither of you have seen that movie?" Janice shook her head, an expression of humor and dismay on her face; she wore that look a lot around us.

Usually, William and I did a good job of keeping Janice on task, but when she'd veered toward *Casablanca* tonight, William couldn't help himself. Apparently, he thought himself a modern-day Humphrey Bogart. Not as an actor, but as a hard-boiled but ultimately good guy who rescues damsels in distress — his words, not mine. With his scrawny frame, I didn't think he could pull himself out of a wet paper bag, let alone another human.

"Just because I wouldn't want to stay in a Vichy-controlled city swarming with German and Italian officials during World War II doesn't mean I haven't had great sex." My voice faltered at the end, not because it wasn't true, but because I didn't want too many people to overhear. It came out sounding insecure.

"When's the last time you experienced The Big O?" Janice nudged me. She didn't seem at all flustered that she was grilling me about my sex life during a study session.

"Not since Meg, I'm guessing. Which was what? A year ago? Longer?" William said. "And I'm sorry, but it's hard to believe Meg was a giver. A taker, maybe, but not a giver. And The Big O ... I don't see it with her. Not with her — "

The table jumped an inch off the floor. Janice must've really walloped William in the shins.

"Why are you kicking me? It's no secret that Meg and Lizzie used to date and that Meg — "

There was another scuffle under the table. Janice knew much more than William, and it'd become typical for her to act like my protective older sister.

I rolled my eyes. "Can we get back to business?" I flicked the pages of the three books we had to read for this week's seminars. "I'm sure Dr. Marcel won't ask any questions about The Big O.

Only Goebbels, Himmler, and Göring will be up for discussion."

All of us studied World War II, concentrating on Nazi Germany. Our current reading seminar focused on the rise of the Third Reich and the leaders who'd made it possible.

"Now Joseph Goebbels, don't get me wrong or misinterpret what I'm about to say, since we all know he was evil" – Janice shifted in her seat – "but with his position as the Reich's Minister of Propaganda and the way he coerced actresses to date him, he was probably better in the sack. Yeah, he had a clubfoot, but I don't think that would have impeded him much. Hermann Göring, maybe during his WWI ace flying days, before he ballooned out and became addicted to morphine … but Heinrich Himmler, the scrawny former chicken farmer" – she shook her head – "that man was never a good lay."

This was why I didn't think it was a good idea to mix booze with studies. Two hours earlier everyone was focused. Now, Janice was wandering into dangerous territory.

To my amazement, William joined the discussion. "What about Hitler?" he asked without moving his lips. It had taken me days, if not weeks, to get used to that quirk of his, yet I still caught myself staring at his mouth from time to time.

"Hitler?" Janice's voice cracked. "No way. I bet he couldn't even get it up. Besides, didn't he only have one ball?"

"That's the theory. Apparently, the Soviets chopped off one of his nuts and it's somewhere in Russia." William raised his eyebrows. He had a long, narrow face and a sloped forehead, and the gesture made him resemble a cartoon character.

"I've heard he liked to play dress-up and ask, 'Do I look like the Führer?'" Janice giggled and then took a sip of her beer.

I groaned.

"That reminds me." She swiveled to face me. "You never answered my question."

I stared at her.

"Your last Big O?" She smiled. "Including when it was just you." Her exaggerated wink made me roll my eyes.

William's eyes glimmered with too much interest. Shit, that reminded me to get cash before next week's session. Knowing Meg, she'd follow through on her threat of spilling all the juicy details about our sex life. Not that we had much sex in the final months. Meg was usually passed out drunk each and every night.

Not answering, I started shoving books into my bag.

Janice peered at her watch. "Oh, crap. I'm late meeting friends for dinner. See ya in class tomorrow." Unencumbered by books or a bag, she made a quick escape.

William stood and stretched. I eyed his silk patchwork belt, which featured whales, fish, and crabs. His blue gingham Vineyard Vines shirt was untucked at the back. He crammed his books and notebook into a leather briefcase more suited to Indiana Jones than to a history grad student and then raised one hand. I wasn't sure if he was gesturing good-bye or motioning me not to speak. Then he spun on his heel and marched out.

I shook my head and made my exit. Outside, I unlocked my bike from the overcrowded rack and hopped on. It was dark, but it was only eight o'clock, so I still had time to cram in a few hours of work before crashing and waking at six for my morning ride.

It didn't take long to reach my apartment. I hung my Cannondale from the hooks in the entryway ceiling, walked past the bookshelves and stacks of paperbacks that inhabited every available space, and veered off to the side of the main room to a small dining room that doubled as my office. The books offset the starkness of the cotton-white walls and institutional-beige carpet in my one-bedroom apartment. They were the only personal touches since I was never big on photos or decorating. Who had the time for trivial matters?

There was no one to greet me. I lived alone, and had done so since Meg left. Not that Meg and I had officially lived together, but when we were dating, she had stayed over many nights. Besides weekly meetings with colleagues and a meet-up with my buddy Ethan at Starbucks once a week, most of my human interaction took place on campus. I taught classes three times a week, attended seminars, and held office hours twice a week. During holidays and school breaks, I could go for days without speaking to anyone. I'd always felt more comfortable around books, which was why even the walls of the hallway and bedroom were lined with shelves.

I wasn't close to my family, which was okay with everyone on both sides. I didn't like them, and they didn't approve of me. My mother loved to refer to me as "the Les-Bi-An," never her daughter. My father was silent. And my older brother, Peter, was too busy getting rich on the West Coast and conjuring up ways to steal my inheritance.

In the kitchen, I prepared my usual two ham and cheese sandwiches, snatched a banana and an apple from the fruit bowl, and rummaged around for a large bag of tortilla chips and hummus. Then I settled in at the dining room table. Time to get some research done for my Hitler Youth dissertation, which analyzed the youth movement that indoctrinated young boys so they would grow up to be perfect Nazi soldiers. I had been slaving away in grad school for the past few years, and my current goal was to finish my dissertation in two years. My advisor was convinced I needed at least three, but I'd show him. I'd completed my undergrad in three and a half years with a double major in history and politics and flew through my master's in two.

Still, the huge stack of books on the table elicited a sigh, which, for a brief moment, I was certain echoed through my apartment.

"DO YOU THINK I'm pathetic?" I asked Ethan as he added gobs of sugar to his Starbucks house blend.

He dipped his head almost a foot and peered at me through his spectacles. "How am I supposed to answer that?"

"Honestly. Do you think I'm pathetic?"

Ethan maneuvered his lanky frame past three untidy tables and I followed, grimacing at the messiness of the place, until we settled on one that was almost clean. It was a little after ten on Saturday, and although it was quiet now, the early morning rush must have taken the staff by surprise. Two teenagers leaned against the counter, dazed and confused.

"Okay, what's got your panties in a bunch this morning?" Ethan set down his coffee, took off his coke-bottle thick glasses, and cleaned them with a cloth.

"The other night, William and Janice got on my case about how long it's been since I experienced The Big O." I didn't bother whispering the last part. Aside from the employees behind the counter, the place was deserted.

"The Big O?" He hitched up one of his thin eyebrows.

"You know. In bed."

"Oh, you mean the last time you had an orgasm." He wiped both eyes with his fingers before replacing his glasses. "And?"

"And what?"

He snorted. "When was the last time?"

I scratched my chin. "Not sure really. Meg."

"That was well over a year ago."

"Good grief. Not you as well. For someone who doesn't like sex, I didn't think you would gang up on me, too."

"Gang up on you?" He laughed. "I'm just curious." He ignored my comment about not liking sex. With the exception of coffee, Ethan disliked fluids of all types, but especially bodily fluids. It made me wonder how he'd managed to get married.

"And their comments got you thinking?" he added.

"Yes. I mean no. Maybe," I stammered. "I just keep thinking about it."

"About what? The Big O or not having anyone in your life?" As usual, Ethan hit the nail on the head.

"Just the other day, I ran into one of my former professors. This guy is ancient, in a wheelchair, and he smells like an old person who's about to move on to the next world. Out of the blue he started telling me about how he and his lady friend went to the movies. I was flabbergasted. How did he have a lady friend? I don't even have a pet. Not even a goldfish."

"Do you want a lady friend?" Ethan's tone bordered on teasing.

"I don't know. Maybe. It might be nice to have someone." I peered out the window and watched the commotion taking place on College Avenue. "Most days I'm fine, but ..."

"My advice. Don't search for it. If you try to find a girlfriend, it won't happen. But if you're at peace with your life, it'll happen naturally, sooner rather than later."

"Naturally." I bobbed my head and repeated the word. "Is that how it happened with Lisa?"

He beamed. "Yes and no. We've known each other all our lives. I was so young I didn't even know I was looking." He laughed. "*C'est la vie.*"

"What if I meet someone who turns out to be another Meg?" The thought was more than unsettling; it was horrifying.

Ethan patted my arm. "Not everyone is like Meg. I know trust isn't your biggest strength, but you need to learn to let people in. Not everyone is out to hurt you."

I huffed. "Hurt me?" Ethan knew my relationship with Meg wasn't great, but he didn't have full disclosure. No one did. I couldn't confide in anyone about how bad it had gotten before I reached my breaking point. That night she'd gone way too far. I massaged my lower jaw.

He swatted the air. "Oh, I forgot. You're Lizzie-the-Indestructible." His carefully guarded Southern accent slipped in. Ethan hailed from Mississippi, but most of the time he controlled his twang.

I forced a laugh. "Whatever."

His moustache curled up with his smile. "Having someone in your life could be a good thing. You can't spend all your time with books or riding your bike. Human interaction — have you heard of it?"

Chapter Two

ON MONDAY, I FINISHED EARLY. I'd already had a one-hour Western Civ lecture at eight, followed by two fifty-minute reading discussions before noon. At one o'clock, I attended Dr. Marcel's twentieth-century European history class as the graduate teacher's assistant, and I held office hours from two to four. By half past four, I was usually ready to jump on my bike and head home.

This morning, when I'd left a little after six for my normal forty-five minute bike ride, the sky had been dark as midnight. Around the tenth mile, the sky lightened and I could see half-bare tree branches against the gunmetal sky. Temperatures in northern Colorado at this time of year hovered between the thirties and forties in the early hours, which made for chilly but not unbearable rides. The heavy low-hanging clouds had spurred me to get going before flakes started to fly.

The snow had already melted as I suspected it would. I owned a car, but my preferred method of transportation was my bike. If I didn't ride each day, I was more stressed than usual, and I was already wound way too tight, according to Ethan.

"Lizzie, do you have a minute?"

I forced down an urge to refuse my mentor. Dr. Marcel was a gifted historian, and I was lucky to be under his tutelage. Ten students in the program had applied to work with him, and he'd chosen me after I completed the requirements for my master's. I could still remember the day I received the news. I knew I'd have to work my ass off, and the challenge hadn't terrified me at all. I thrived under pressure.

What I didn't know was how much of a chatterbox Dr. Marcel could be. Every time he asked me into his office, I lost hours. Typically, I didn't mind — after all, he was one of the greatest historians west of the Mississippi. But my plan was to enjoy a rare afternoon bike ride and then fine-tune a lecture for the following week. I preferred to stay a week ahead, and I had to work on an outline for my semester research project, which was due in two weeks. My PhD program was a twenty-four hour job eight days a week. I simply didn't have time for Dr. Marcel this afternoon.

"Of course, Dr. Marcel," I said as sweetly as I could, trying to quash my unease.

"I'd like you to meet Sarah Cavanaugh." Dr. Marcel motioned to a young woman sitting in a leather librarian chair inside his plush office.

She was stunning. Chin-length chestnut-brown hair framed her face, highlighting her penetrating chocolate eyes and alabaster skin. Worries about my lecture and paper slipped into the recesses of my mind.

"Hello." She stood to shake my hand. Her skin was soft, and I thought I detected a hint of lavender.

"Hi, Ms. Cavanaugh." I dipped my head slightly and smoothed the front of my sweater-vest, which had a habit of bunching and giving the illusion of a potbelly.

She colored. "Sarah is just fine. I don't even like it when my students call me Ms. Cavanaugh."

"Oh, do you teach here?"

How in the world had I not met this gorgeous professor? I needed to get my head out of my books — and out of my ass.

"Sarah teaches English at a local high school," Dr. Marcel interjected. "She's on a committee to inspire more high school grads to attend college." He stopped speaking, giving the impression I now knew the reason for the introduction.

"That's wonderful," I said, unclear as to why I was needed for this meeting. I was a grad student, not an admissions officer.

I think she understood my predicament. My eyes had a way of betraying every emotion. "Our plan is to bring a handful of students to campus for a day. Have them sit in on some classes to give them a taste of college life." Sarah smiled awkwardly.

"Unfortunately, the plan is for them to visit next Wednesday, and my class is scheduled to take an exam." Dr. Marcel continued to beam vaguely, like the lovable village idiot.

I knew all about the exam; I was the one who'd written all the questions and would be doing all the grading. Graduate students were, in reality, indentured servants to the top professors in the department.

"I'm hoping you'll agree, Lizzie." Dr. Marcel's grin lit up the room.

"Agree?" My voice cracked and flashes of heat crept up my face.

"For my students to sit in on your class," explained Sarah. Her voice was sweet, magnetically so.

"Oh, yes, of course!" My sudden enthusiasm embarrassed me, but Dr. Marcel seemed to appreciate it. Sarah elevated one eyebrow in such a way that I thought for sure she was trying to decide whether I was mentally unstable or a blathering simpleton like my portly but kind mentor. Surely she was used to affecting people this way — men and women.

Would it be too obvious if I released my hair from the

ubiquitous ponytail holder that was tightly twisted several times, strangling the thin strands into compliance? I imagined flirtatiously tossing it about like in the movies.

"Great." Dr. Marcel joined his hands together as if he were praying and nodded his head absently. Anyone who didn't know him would have thought he was senile, but he had one of the sharpest minds and never put on airs. He could lecture for more than an hour without any notes, and his information was always spot-on. During my first year, I tried catching him in a falsehood, or even just a wrong date or name. It never happened. He swiveled his head to me and then to Sarah. "That's wonderful."

All three of us stood in his office, unsure where to go from there.

Finally, Sarah eased the tension. "Would you have time later this week to go over the plans?"

"I'm free this evening," I blurted.

"Uh," she uttered.

I put up one palm. "Of course, you probably have plans. Later this week works as well. Whenever. I'm at your beck and call." I wrenched at my collar to release the heat pouring off my face and neck. Why was I insistent on acting like a fool in front of this woman?

"Are you available now for a quick cup of coffee?" she asked.

"Yes!" *Seriously, Lizzie. Bring it down a peg or two.*

"Wonderful," Dr. Marcel said, not noticing that his star doctoral student transformed into a complete and total loser around a beautiful woman. I wasn't the smoothest person, but I usually had more composure in the workplace. Not around Sarah, apparently.

We said our good-byes to the professor and made our way to the student center.

My brain was going a mile a minute trying to come up with

something witty to say. Nothing came to mind. It was as if a loose screw had flown into my mental machinery, causing a total system failure. Instead of speaking, I stared at the ground as we walked, wondering whether each step was quashing my chance of asking her on a date.

"I really appreciate you taking the time out of your schedule." Sarah threw me a bone.

"Not at all. The pleasure is all mine. How do you like teaching high school students?" *Really, I could only come up with a work question?*

"I love it. My tenth graders are challenging, but most days I enjoy it. Of course, it must be different teaching college students." Her full lips turned up into a smile, beckoning mine.

"I doubt it. I teach freshmen. Half of the students are either falling asleep or texting. The rest are still in bed." Then I remembered I was supposed to impress her students. "But I'll amp up my lecture for you."

She laughed. "Good to know things don't change much."

The sparkle in her eyes made me wonder whether she could be interested in a stodgy PhD student. Why did I have to dress so much like an uptight grad student today?

She ordered a coffee, and I opted for a chai.

"I've never tried a chai before. What's it like?" she asked when we took our seats.

I gaped at her as if she was speaking Latin. *Never tried a chai?* "Uh, it's quite good." I started to laugh. "I'm sorry. I'm not making a very good impression, am I?"

Sarah shook her head seductively. "It's kinda cute actually."

That emboldened me a little. "Here. Taste it for yourself." I handed her my drink.

She took a sip, nodded appreciatively, and then took another sip.

"You can keep it if you want." Again, searing heat seeped into my cheeks, and I thought my skull would crack from the intensity.

"You don't mind?" She raised both eyebrows.

"Not at all."

"What else can I get you to do for me?" she asked in a flirty tone.

"You name it." I hoped I sounded confident, not pleading.

"Hmmm ... anything?" She tapped her manicured fingertips on the table, pretending to be deep in thought.

"Shall we start with dinner?" My voice sounded odd, probably because I wasn't breathing as I spoke.

She chuckled. "That sounds like a good start. When?"

This woman didn't mess around. I liked that about her. "Friday?" I asked, accidentally dragging out each syllable.

"Maybe. But first, we should talk about next Wednesday." Her body language switched from seductive to professional.

The giddiness leached out of my body. "Of course," I said with as much conviction as possible. "Hit me with your plan."

She smiled at that and then launched into the program and her role. "A recent study has shown the number of high school graduates who go on to college is declining. Our goal is to help students learn more about their options, including scholarships, work-study programs, and loans since the Great Recession has made it harder for some parents to help out their children by remortgaging their homes or whatnot. And to encourage them to go above and beyond to find ways to seek responsible funding, we want them to get a taste of college life to show them what they'll be missing. We've scheduled a tour, a couple class visits, a lunch with faculty members and student ambassadors, meetings with admissions and financial aid, and we'll even visit fraternity and sorority houses — not parties, of course."

Sarah continued discussing the program and dropping alarming statistics. I could tell she had the spiel down to an art form. And that she truly cared about the kids in her group. "It's a new program, and I hope next year to double the amount of interested students."

I nodded encouragingly all the while imagining her naked.

"What do you think?" Sarah said after her shtick.

I grinned enthusiastically. Not only did I think her plan was excellent, but I wanted to get her to agree to a date. If I thought it would help my cause, I would dip into my trust fund to set up a scholarship fund for the program. It had been a long time since I felt myself this drawn to a woman. And truth be known, it confused the hell out of me. What had happened to the PhD student who preferred being surrounded by books? Now, I was envisioning her legs wrapped around me.

"Sounds great. Sign me up." That was stupid since I'd already agreed for her students to attend my class.

Sarah glanced at her watch. Her wrist was delicate, her skin creamy. "Oh, look at the time. I'm meeting someone in less than an hour." She retrieved a business card and pen from her purse. "Here, this is my cell number. Call me about Friday." With that, she hopped out of her seat and rushed off. I didn't even have time to say good-bye.

I wondered who she was meeting.

Chapter Three

A LITTLE AFTER FIVE, A knock on my office door caused a million butterflies to flutter in my stomach like it was the end of summer, and they knew they didn't have much time left. Via text, Sarah and I had made plans to meet at my office on Friday evening, when she said she had to be on campus anyway. Or maybe she just hadn't wanted me to know where she lived. Not giving out my address was something I would do. We'd only talked that one day and texted a few times, but I got the feeling Sarah was an open book. Not only was I a closed book, but I also had reinforced padlocks securely attached.

"Come in," I called, straightening my hair.

Sarah popped her lovely head around the door. "You ready?" she asked, making it clear we would be vacating my office immediately. Being a grad student meant my office was one of the worst rooms in the history wing, if not the worst room. It was barely larger than a closet and had a fusty, cellar smell. "Of course." I grabbed my jacket. "Where are you parked?"

"Can we take your car? Mine broke down this morning, so my mom had to drop me off." She smiled sheepishly.

"Sure." I motioned for her to take a left down the hallway. "I hope it's nothing serious." Thank goodness I hadn't ridden my bike this morning. I didn't want to smell like dried sweat for my big date. *Big date. Get a hold of yourself, Lizzie.* It was just dinner with a stunning woman. That was all.

She let out a puff of air. "I'm afraid it's time for a new one."

Not knowing what to say, I opened the door to the stairwell and motioned for her to go ahead. We were on the fourth floor, but after descending two flights, I led us down a dark hallway.

"Where are you taking me? This is creepy." She reached for my hand.

"A secret passage. Trust me, nothing will happen to you."

She whirled around. "That's a shame."

I squeezed her hand, and her smile made me wet. I didn't know whether I was coming or going around her. "Right here." I opened a door to another stairwell. Two flights down, another door led to the parking lot and to my car.

"Nice spot!"

"It helps that not many know about that hallway. So don't tell." I flashed my best million-dollar smile.

"Your secret is safe with me. For a price."

I unlocked the door of my Toyota Camry, which had seen better days as the missing hubcap attested, and opened it. "Really? What's your fee?"

"I haven't decided yet." She slid into the seat and shut the door in my face.

I definitely liked her style.

I got into the car and flipped the key in the ignition, immediately regretting it as a voice blasted over the speakers. I tried to punch the eject button on the CD player, but Sarah slapped my hand away.

"What are you listening to?"

"Uh, a book," I said.

Her eyebrows shot so high they almost reached the top of

her skull. "Get out!" She continued to swat my hand away. It took some doing, but I was able to turn the volume down all the way. "What book?"

"*The Rise and Fall of the Third Reich*," I said in a tiny voice.

Sarah flashed me a knowing, rather baffling smile. "I like that about you." Without further explanation, she fiddled with the radio. Soon, music streamed through the speakers. I didn't recognize the woman singing, but I was grateful for the distraction. I was certain I was the first woman Sarah had dated who listened to audiobooks in the car, and ones about the Nazis to boot; however, I wasn't brimming with confidence that it created the best impression on a first date.

Somehow I was able to concentrate on driving, even while mortified by the audiobook debacle and her mystifying smile. "Where shall we go?"

"Do you like Vietnamese?"

"I know of a place on Drake."

She slapped my leg. "That's the one I was thinking of." Instead of removing her hand, she left it resting on my thigh.

Luckily, it was a short drive. Having her so near, touching me, was sending my body into a tizzy. I envisioned wrecking the car and her mom having to drive both of us home — probably not the best first impression to make with her mother. Moms didn't like me much. Mine despised me, and my ex's mom had wanted to rip my head off for turning her daughter into a lesbian. I hadn't turned Meg, but I was the first woman she'd introduced to her family. That was pretty much all the experience I had with mothers. Dating had never been very high on my to-do list. I suppressed a chuckle as I imagined such a list: pick up requested items from the library, grade exams, pursue an attractive woman, edit journal article. Truth be told, I was such a dedicated student that even if I did have it on my agenda, it would have been repeatedly pushed to the bottom. Until I met Sarah.

The hostess seated us at a booth in the nearly deserted restaurant that resembled an Asian version of IHOP. Each setting had a paper placemat with a Vietnamese map. The food more than made up for the lackluster interior and harsh lighting.

Frigid temperatures and razor-sharp wind outside had clearly kept most people home. Winter hadn't officially arrived, but someone forgot to inform Mother Nature.

"I swear this place is usually hopping," Sarah said.

I surveyed the room. "Yeah, sure," I said lightheartedly. "I get to pick the next place."

"Next place, huh? Do you always make assumptions on a first date?" Her tone suggested there would be another date, but her dark eyes were harder to read.

A waiter approached to take our drink order.

Sarah winked at me and whispered, "Safe, for now."

That made me smile.

I ordered a Thai tea; Sarah, the house red.

My phone vibrated in the left pocket of my trousers, and my leg jerked involuntarily against the table, nearly spilling my water. I resisted the urge to see who it was. Technology wasn't my thing, and people only called or texted me when trouble was brewing, or in Meg's case, when she needed money. However, I always had my outdated flip phone on, unless I was in class.

"You okay?" asked Sarah, craning her neck over the menu.

I nodded, ignoring the situation to the best of my ability.

Sarah let it go. "Shall we get an appetizer?" she asked with the sincerest look on her face. Was this a test?

I nodded enthusiastically. "Yes, please. It's been a long time since" — I was going to say *since I had a meal that wasn't a sandwich*, but I changed it to — "since I've been here."

She ordered the appetizer combo, which included fried

shrimp, two egg rolls, and steamed dumplings. My mouth watered.

My phone buzzed again. This time, I controlled my leg so it didn't whack the table. Right then, Sarah said she needed to use the bathroom. As soon as she was out of sight, I checked my messages. Dr. Marcel had called and texted twice, telling me he had to go out of town for an emergency and asking if I could teach his class on Monday. I quickly responded *yes* and to let me know if he needed anything else. As I punched in the last letter, Sarah was already heading back to the table. I anxiously hit send and surreptitiously slipped the phone into my pocket. I didn't want to give her the impression I was glued to my phone. Ironically, I had only recently learned how to text after Ethan poked fun at my texting incompetence. Luckily, Sarah hadn't seemed to notice.

The waiter arrived with the appetizers, plunked the plate down in the center, and then backed away, bowing subserviently.

"Thanks," I said, unsure whether I should clasp my hands together and bow. *Wait, isn't that a Japanese tradition, not Vietnamese?*

"You trying to solve world peace over there?" asked Sarah. She expertly plucked up a dumpling with her chopsticks and dipped half of it into the soy sauce.

"World peace? No." I smiled awkwardly. "Just trying to remember Asian etiquette."

"You can use a fork if necessary." She tilted her head toward the silverware, missing my point completely.

I laughed. "Do you think I'm a barbarian or something?"

She held another dumpling in the air. "Prove me wrong."

I snapped the wooden chopsticks apart and rubbed the area where they had been conjoined, eliminating any snags, which always bothered me. With my eyes on Sarah, I deftly picked up a dumpling, praying my shaking hands wouldn't betray me.

"There," I said.

"Go on. Dip it." She teased me.

I did, but before I could place it in my mouth, Sarah accidentally knocked over the sriracha hot chile bottle and it rolled into my lap. My dumpling popped out of my chopsticks and hit the table, splattering soy sauce all over my shirt.

"You cheated!" I stabbed the sticks in her direction and then fished the hot sauce from my crotch.

Sarah sniggered. "It slipped." She gave a mock shrug.

"Yeah, right. That was sabotage, pure and simple."

"We should have made a wager." Sarah's wrinkled forehead told me she'd never confess resorting to devious machinations.

"I'd be a fool to bet against you. You have no honor."

"Take that back." She jabbed her chopsticks toward my heart.

"Will not." I parried her sticks with my own as if we were dueling with swords. Sarah bravely fought back.

The waiter began to approach, but then froze, clearly baffled by our childish behavior.

We giggled, and set our weapons aside as the waiter whisked away the rest of the uneaten appetizers without uttering a word. Damn! I was hungry.

"I think we're in trouble," Sarah whispered.

"Totally improper Vietnamese etiquette to have a chopsticks clash at the table." I winked.

Sarah covered her mouth to stifle a snort. The waiter was already hurrying back with our main course, probably in the hope we'd bolt our food down and make a mad dash for our car.

During dinner, the weather worsened. Snowflakes swirled furiously, creating a soupy mess of the sidewalk.

Sarah stared out the window, a dreamy expression on her face. "There aren't many who could get me out on a date on a night like this." She dipped a spoon into her beef rice-noodle soup. I had opted for the beef rice bowl.

"That's Colorado for you. Unpredictable weather. Unfortunately, I can't promise nice weather for our next date either." I clacked my chopsticks in the air, happy that my shakiness was at a minimum thanks to the meds.

"So, there *will* be another date."

Placing my hand over hers, I then pressed it comfortingly. "That, I can promise."

"Now, here's the real test." She narrowed her eyes before continuing. "Shall we get dessert?"

"By all means, or what's the point of going out to eat?"

Her approving nod told me I'd answered correctly. "I like a woman who isn't afraid to eat."

It made me laugh. Sarah was slender, so I was surprised she wanted appetizers and dessert. I had a super-duper metabolism thanks to my Graves' disease, so I could eat everything on the menu and not gain an ounce.

"Ice cream or mini cheesecakes?"

"Why limit ourselves?" I spun around to the waiter and ordered the green-tea ice cream and cheesecake.

His fake smile spoke volumes. He wanted us gone, but he was too polite to say so. Another person kept poking his head out of the kitchen. I got the impression that once we left, they'd close for the night.

With the increasingly nasty weather outside, we didn't linger long after we polished off dessert. When the waiter set the bill down in the middle of the table, we both reached for it.

"You have enough going on with your car. Please, let me pay," I said.

"Only if you let me pick up the next time."

"Okay, but this could be a never-ending cycle." I smiled.

"Would that be a bad thing?" She seemed so relaxed, even though this was our first date. An uncomfortable tightness settled in my chest.

Sarah asked me to drop her off at her mom's, where she was staying until she figured out the car situation. Sitting in the car in her mother's driveway, I suddenly felt like a teenager. "Um ..." *Should I say I'll call you?*

Sarah laughed, leaned over, and kissed my cheek. "Thanks for dinner. I'll call you."

The lights outside the house lit up as if it was Times Square. The water droplets on the windshield reflected the lights, making me feel as if I was under the lights in a police interrogation room. "I think your mom knows you're home."

"You think?" She shook her head, smiling. "Seriously, I'll call you."

"Not if I call you first," I yelled after her as she walked to the front door. Sarah circled around and stared for a second before retreating inside. *Really? Did I have to be such a moron all the time?*

I waited for a moment, just in case she forgot something.

She didn't.

The clock on my dashboard said it was eight. Our date was a short one. Was that a good or bad sign? I hunched over the steering wheel to get a better view of the sky. *Stupid snow.*

My stomach grumbled. Putting the car in reverse, I decided to treat myself by stopping at Taco Bell before heading home.

Chapter Four

TWO WEEKS LATER, SARAH CALLED. We'd seen each other briefly the day when her students sat in on my class, and we'd exchanged a few texts since our date, but I hadn't heard her voice in over a week. As soon as I did, I relaxed.

"Do you want to get together for coffee on Thursday night?"

"Sure." If she'd asked me to go hunting for crocodiles stark-naked I would have readily agreed.

"I'm so sorry it took me this long to call," she said. "My schedule has been jam-packed. I promise to make it up to you."

She had a sexy phone voice, and I wished I had the courage to ask if that meant I'd be seeing her naked soon. Instead, I replied, "Can't wait."

"TELL ME, LIZZIE, who knows you better than anyone else?" Sarah asked and then broke off a piece of blueberry muffin and popped it in her mouth. She'd suggested a coffee shop around the corner from my office, a quaint place that reminded me of a cozy kitchen in colonial America rather than a modern-day joint.

Finding the question odd, I took my time answering. "Ethan," I said eventually, with no intention of elaborating. Me, secretive? Absolutely.

"What's he like?" She blew into her mocha latte.

I blurted out, "He doesn't like sex."

Sarah flinched. "Oh, did you two date?"

"What? No!" I blinked several times, trying to delete the mental image from my head. "No, we're just good friends." I tugged on the collar of my wool sweater. "I'm not sure why I spilled the beans about that. It's not like he goes around telling everyone." *Lizzie, stop rambling, you idiot!*

Sarah smiled sweetly. Too sweetly. Like I was a special needs kid.

It was making me uncomfortable. "Usually, I'm pretty good at keeping secrets."

Sarah let out a bark of laughter. "Thanks for the warning."

"I didn't mean it like that. I meant other people's secrets." I yanked my sweater off as casually as possible.

She slid her hand onto my leg under the table. "Getting a little warm?" Her fingers fondled my thigh. "Relax. You aren't in trouble."

"That may be true, but I'm not scoring any points either," I said in all seriousness.

"Are you trying to?" Her eyes twinkled.

"No. I mean yes, but you aren't supposed to know that." I nibbled on my bottom lip and tasted mint Chapstick. I never wore lipstick, but I'd applied some eye shadow and a touch of mascara moments before meeting Sarah.

"Says who?"

She had me there. It was becoming apparent to both of us that dating wasn't my specialty. If I were Sarah, I'd be racking my brain for an excuse to bail, and then I'd change my phone number.

I shrugged.

"I bet if I asked you to cite three reasons why you study

history, you would be able to do so without hesitation."

"It's the greatest story — "

She put a palm in the air. "There. Now you're more relaxed."

It was true. All of a sudden my awkwardness had oozed out of me — well, at least 60 percent of it. I wiggled my head, trying to dislodge the other 40 percent. It didn't work.

"How about you? Who knows everything about you?"

"My mom."

I laughed ... until I realized she was serious. "Oh, that's cool." My relaxed feeling started to ebb. I couldn't fathom telling my mom my favorite color let alone anything super-duper private. Nerves chewed their way back into my stomach, and I took a long tug of chai to quell them. "Are you hungry?"

Are you hungry? That was the only thing I could think of? I saw a big flashing red sign over Sarah's head: *Mayday! Mayday!* Followed by an image of me hurtling through the sky without a parachute.

Narrowing her eyes, she said, "Yeah, this muffin tastes like sandpaper." She pushed the plate away. "Where would you like to go? My treat."

I waggled a finger at her. "You paid for the drinks. If I remember correctly, you set the rules. It's my turn."

"Nicely played. Maybe you aren't a complete amateur." Color pricked her high cheekbones, and I suspected she hadn't meant to verbalize the second sentence.

I couldn't stop myself from laughing. "Only time will tell. Tell me, do many of your dates stay one step ahead of you? I feel like I'm consistently three steps behind." I leaned closer. "Of course, I like the view."

She swatted my arm. "I can't believe you." Her expression told me I'd finally scored a point. "Just for that, I'm picking the place for dinner."

"Fine by me." I stood and put out my hand to help her up.

"Where to?"

Twenty minutes later, the hostess at an Italian bistro led us to a secluded table in the back of a dimly lit romantic hotspot — or so it seemed, since all the tables were filled with couples that only had eyes for each other. Sarah walked in front of me, the exaggerated sway in her step strained the pencil skirt provocatively, doing wonders for my libido. She casually rubbernecked over her shoulder to see if I was enjoying the show. Indeed I was. I hoped my foolish smirk let her know it.

After taking our drink orders, the server left us.

"Do you ever drink?" asked Sarah, placing a linen napkin over her lap.

"Not when I'm driving. One whiff and I'm drunk. On occasion, I enjoy a rum and Coke in the comfort of my own home."

"I'll have to remember that."

"Planning on taking advantage of me?" I asked in my most seductive tone.

"Do I have to? I saw the way you were checking out my ass." Her sexy, almost imperceptible grin made me yearn for more.

"Wasn't that what you were going for?" Two could play at this game.

"Maybe."

A waiter arrived with Sarah's glass of wine and a Coke for me. He announced the specials before waltzing off to take care of other lovebirds.

Sarah studied the menu. "I think I'll get the harvest squash ravioli. You?" She peered over at me.

"Chicken parmigiana."

"Nice. Hope you don't mind, but I plan on tasting it."

"You can taste anything you want."

She bit her lower lip and continued to peruse the menu. "We

might be in trouble when it comes to the dessert. Have you seen all the goodies on offer?"

My eyes wandered to the smidgeon of cleavage her silk blouse exposed. "Not yet, but I hope to."

Sarah's eyes flashed downward, and then she slowly raised them to meet mine. "I don't think those are on the menu." She took a sip of her wine, watching me carefully and clearly noticing my disappointment. "Not yet, at least."

Not breaking eye contact, I said, "I think you'll find I'm very patient." It took every ounce of chutzpah to sound convincing. If she'd given me any inkling that I might whisk her out of the restaurant and straight to my bed, I would have pushed everyone over to make haste — even the old lady by the door.

The glint in her eye told me she knew it. The truth was Sarah was unlike any woman I had ever met. I had a feeling I was heading for some serious relationship trouble. She wasn't the type who just wanted a roll in the hay. She was the type who wanted love with a capital L. If I wasn't careful, I could fall prey to her charms.

The whole love aspect was new territory for me, really. Even though Meg and I had been together for a couple of years, we weren't all that lovey-dovey. Maybe in the beginning, but now when I reflected, the memories that popped into my mind were filled with turmoil and fear of her having that drink that'd push her over the edge into the mean-Meg zone. Tipsy Meg was flirtatious and fun. Drunk Meg was a scary, vindictive bitch.

Not that I was completely turned off by love. I wanted it. I mean I *would* — if the mere thought didn't make me want to find a secluded cave to live in for the rest of my days. Yet, when I looked into Sarah's soft eyes, I felt the tug of love.

I washed it away with a healthy dose of Coke.

Our small table was arranged so that Sarah and I sat right

next to each other. She placed her hand high up on my leg, settling the panic attack that was forming inside me.

"This could get interesting. Very interesting, indeed," she murmured. Her hand rested between my thighs now, and I wondered if she felt my warmth. I wanted her, no doubt. Sarah was wearing a skirt, and I might have done my own hand inspection if I hadn't had a feeling she wouldn't let me. It wasn't part of her plan, and there was no doubt in my mind she always wanted to hold the winning cards. I was elated, terrified, perplexed. One question kept flitting into my brain: Could Sarah be the one?

I wiped the thought from my mind. It was way too soon for that. Besides, as I'd learned with Meg, people showed their true colors sooner rather than later. *Patience, Lizzie. See where this leads, but don't let your guard down. Ever.*

We finished our meals. "Well, it's that time," she said.

Her teasing smile and squinting eyes made me wonder if she was almost dripping with desire like I was. "What time is that?"

"Time to decide what to devour next." Sarah licked her index finger and then ran the finger over her lips.

At first, I was confused, which was no doubt her intention.

"Oh, dessert," I said, waving at our waiter before requesting a dessert menu. "What sounds good to you?" I asked once the waiter had retreated into the darkness.

"All of it," she murmured, without even glancing at the menu. In fact, I was pretty sure she wasn't talking about dessert. I needed to wrest back some control.

"Then it's decided." I got the waiter's attention again and ordered a sampling of every dessert on the menu.

Sarah didn't speak. She didn't need to. I was scoring points left and right.

"Would you like grappa?" asked the waiter.

"Yes, two please," Sarah answered for me.

I'd never had grappa, but I'd drink gasoline if she asked me to.

It didn't take long for the waiter to return, and I was amazed he was able to fit everything on our quaint little table.

Sarah raised an elegant glass of grappa, waiting for me to reciprocate. "To a chance meeting and to seeing where it goes."

I clinked my glass with hers before taking a sip. The liquor's unpleasant kick made my eyes well up, but I was determined not to show weakness.

Sarah set her drink down and reached for a fork, but I swatted her hand away. "Allow me." I prepared a bite of tiramisu and placed it delicately in her mouth.

"Oooh ... that's good." She wiped her chin with a napkin.

We sipped our grappa again.

Next, I fed her the crème brûlée. The crack of the burnt top promised greatness, and from the moans coming from Sarah, she was in heaven. So was I.

Again, a sip of grappa.

"I think we need more." Sarah snapped her fingers, making me laugh. The waiter, pouring wine for another couple, watched Sarah point to our grappa glasses and raise two slender fingers. He nodded, not at all upset that she was ordering him about. I had a feeling Sarah got her way with almost everyone. The goofy grin on his face made me want to say, *Easy big fella. She's mine.*

"Shall we wait, or is the triple chocolate cheesecake calling your name?" I prepared a tiny portion.

"Whatever you do, Lizzie, don't stop."

I felt my pussy throb, imagining the same conversation in bed. "Anything for you."

Sarah's eyes rolled up in her head. "Oh, that's the best so far."

The waiter set down two more glasses of grappa and left without saying a word. I planned on leaving him a large tip as a thank-you.

"Well, well, well. What do we have here?" If Meg hadn't been standing right in front of me, I would have recognized her snide tone, even despite the fact that she'd dyed her once-blonde hair a rich, fiery red. "Getting drunk on a school night. Shame on you, Lizzie. What would Dr. Marcel say?" Meg's companion helped her slip into a coat. Hopefully, that meant they were leaving and pronto.

Approximately 150,000 people lived in Fort Collins, and the one person I didn't want to bump into ever, let alone with Sarah, was peering down at us.

"Hello," was all I could force out.

Meg's gaze wandered over Sarah's face and upper body before settling on me. "What happened to only drinking at home?" She crossed her arms.

"I'm afraid I'm a bad influence." Sarah came to my defense.

"I see." An older man tugged on Meg's arm. She wore a tight dress — not her usual jeans and J. Crew sweater. And she was with a man — very unusual. "Have a good night, Lizzie." She turned each Z in my name into a weapon. "Oh, I'll be calling you to discuss that financial situation you brought up last time." She gave Sarah a final glare and rolled her eyes. Red-hot anger raged through my mind and body as I clamped my lips together to keep everything bottled inside. How dare she treat Sarah so flippantly?

I counted to ten before I said, "I'm so sorry."

Sarah's eyes darted across the room to where Meg and her companion were exiting into the darkness. "Is she a friend?"

I snorted. "Former ..." I'd been about to say girlfriend, but instead added, "acquaintance."

"I'd use another word for her."

I let out a rush of air. "Really? What would that be?"

"Bitch."

"That one works as well." I smiled.

"What financial situation?"

I shrugged. "No clue. It's not like ... history students are wheeling and dealing." *Accept for the wads of cash I hand over each time Meg texts.*

Sarah eyed me, unsure. "You okay?"

"Absolutely." I forced the fury out of my body.

Sarah placed a palm on my cheek. "Who knew I'd have to protect you on a date?"

"Let's hope that's the first and last time."

"Way back in the day, I was addicted to Tae Bo. I'm sure I'd remember the basics in a pinch." She feigned a jab.

"Maybe you can show me some moves, just in case."

"Honey, I'll show you more than that." She winked, and I was fairly certain it wasn't just the grappa talking.

"Promise."

She kissed my cheek, sealing the deal.

"What about you? Do I have to protect you from any crazies in your life?" I asked.

Sarah started to shake her head, but then blushed. "In high school an ex-boyfriend kept slashing my tires."

"What? Why?"

"I think it was because I dumped him right before prom so I could go with another boy."

"Who?"

"Matt. We dated until I left for college. We're still friends, actually."

"He doesn't mind you're bisexual now."

"Who said I was bi?" Sarah hoisted an eyebrow and crossed her arms, pushing her goodies up in such a way I wanted to rip her clothes off.

"Uh ... my apologies. I just assumed — "

She cut me off. "Relax. I'm just giving you shit. But, no, I'm not bi. Once I figured it out — life was so much easier."

I braced for the dreaded "when did you come out?" bonding question.

Instead, Sarah continued. "Matt was a doll when I told him. He gave me a hug and said 'I know.' Whenever we got close to" — she leaned in — "going all the way, I panicked. Once I blurted, 'I need to make cookies for French class' and left poor Mattie with blue balls the size of coconuts and not for the first time." Sarah laughed.

I needed to erase that image from my mind. "What happened with the guy who slashed your tires?"

"Oh him, he left me alone after Matt found out. Matt was the quarterback, and I think the whole team set the jerk right, if you know what I mean."

I wished I had a Matt who could set Meg right.

By the time we polished off the rest of the mini desserts, including a white-chocolate raspberry cheesecake and a cannoli, I was not only stuffed but also sufficiently drunk. I'd lost count, but thought we had two more rounds.

I paid the check and stood, and immediately the room started to spin.

Sarah draped an arm around my shoulders. "You weren't kidding when you said you get drunk fast." Her arm was stronger than I anticipated.

We made it outside, the cold autumn air sobering me up a little, but not enough to drive. Sarah pulled her cell phone out of her purse and made a call. I was too occupied with leaning against the side of the restaurant, trying to stay upright, to hear a word she said.

Was this what it felt like to be Meg — out of control, not caring about those around her? I pushed Meg from my mind. Sarah had her back to me, but from her body language, I could tell she was smiling. Sweet, caring Sarah. Tonight wasn't about Meg — at least I didn't want it to be. *Focus, Lizzie.* Sarah. It was about Sarah. And me. Me and Sarah. If there was to be a me and Sarah now.

"Okay, our ride is on its way. Are you warm enough?" Sarah cupped her hands and blew into them. "It's colder than a witch's tit."

"A witch's tit." The expression broke me out in hysterics.

Sarah giggled at my expense. "Where shall we take you?" she asked.

"Home."

Shaking her head, she laughed again. "I know. Where do you live?" she enunciated.

I told her my address.

Soon, a Cadillac drove up, and Sarah whisked me into the back seat. The woman behind the wheel was the spitting image of Sarah. Realizing it was her mom's car, I tried to sit up straighter and rubbed my eyes with the back of a hand. Sarah slipped into the front seat and told her mom my address.

Streetlights blurred as we whizzed through Old Town as Sarah and her mom chattered like I wasn't in the car. Given the situation, I appreciated Sarah's effort to shield me from further embarrassment. Occasionally, I noticed her mother checking me out in the rearview mirror, and each time I pretended to be riveted with their prattle; however, everything around me was twirling in super slow motion, and I didn't have a clue what they were discussing. I prayed she wouldn't ask me a question. I sensed I had a silly smirk on my face, but try as I might, I couldn't wipe it off.

We had arrived at the restaurant around seven, but when I peeked at my Timex sports watch, I saw it was almost midnight. Thank God it was Thursday, which meant I only had to stumble through one lecture the following day.

When we arrived, Sarah helped me out of the car. Before shutting the door, she said, "I'll be right back, Mom."

I mumbled "Thank you" to her mother, even though I was sure she couldn't hear, since we were already five wobbly steps away from the car.

With one arm wrapped around my waist, Sarah helped me stumble up the stairs. "Where's the kitchen?" she asked when we were inside and tottered off in the direction of my pointed finger as I slumped on the couch. She returned with a Nalgene water bottle I kept in the fridge.

She shook it. "By morning, this should all be gone," she instructed. "Trust me, you'll thank me." With that, she kissed my cheek and said good-bye. I stumbled to my bathroom, peeled off all my clothes, and sat on the toilet — and that was the last thing I remembered.

Chapter Five

THE BLEEP OF A TEXT message jarred me awake. I sat up in bed, completely naked and befuddled. I wasn't the type to sleep naked, not unless I had company. And I hadn't had company in months. I hoisted the covers off my bed, searching for another naked body. There wasn't one. Rubbing the sleep from my eyes, I tried to piece together what had happened the night before.

I read the text from Sarah: *Are you up, drunkie?*

Drunkie? Murkiness clouded my vision, and no matter how hard I tried, I couldn't shake it. Closing one eye, I was able to punch in the three letters for *yes*. Less than a minute later, the phone rang.

"Morning," I answered. My voice sounded much thicker than normal.

"Good morning. I wanted to make sure you didn't sleep in and miss your class."

"What happened?" I massaged my right temple.

"Grappa."

"Grandpa?" I asked, even more bewildered.

She laughed. "No, grappa. It's an Italian brandy."

Brandy. I didn't drink brandy. Not even the Italian kind.

Then, things slowly started to come back to me. I remembered sitting in a restaurant with Sarah. Meg. And then ...

"Oh, God. Your mom." I slapped my forehead.

"No worries. Mom actually thought you were cute, in a drunken buffoon kinda way."

Drunken buffoon! Definitely not the image I wanted to cultivate. "I'm so embarrassed."

"Don't be. It was nice to see you completely relaxed. We may have to do a repeat performance — after you recover, of course."

"You mean I didn't blow it?" I realized too late how pathetic that sounded. With Meg and the grappa, I was shocked Sarah still wanted to meet up again.

"Not one bit. I had a great night." I could hear the smile in her voice. "Do you need a ride to work?"

"Thanks, but I can ride my bike and then pick up my car in Old Town after class."

"You sure you can manage on your bike?"

"I think fresh air will help clear the bubbles in my head." I shook my head, but the movement was unsuccessful in clearing the fuzz.

"Bubbles. Never heard a hangover referred to that way." She laughed. "Don't get sick."

At first I thought she meant don't catch a cold, but the gurgling queasiness in my stomach told me otherwise. "Hopefully I won't. I really can't remember the last time I got soused."

"Soused! I love it. Next time, only virgin daiquiris for you." The playfulness in her voice made me feel better.

"Deal. Thanks for calling."

"Text me when you get to your office so I know you're still alive."

"Will do." The line went dead. It was well after six. Slowly, I made it to the bathroom, holding onto the walls all the way, and carefully stepped into the shower. The hot water revived me, but

I was still dreading the bike ride to campus, let alone giving a lecture. Thank God I had all my notes and PowerPoint slides prepared. I stood under the stream of hot water, chanting, "Just get through your lecture." Afterwards, I could call it a day and go back to bed.

"GOOD MORNING, LIZZIE."

I nodded to Dr. Marcel as we both stood awkwardly in the hallway. He cleared his throat, and I realized he wanted to speak to me. I hoped my voice wouldn't sound as booze-thick as it had when I'd spoken to Sarah earlier. The alcohol had worked its way through my system, but the nausea hadn't. I tilted my head, inviting him to speak.

"If it's okay with you, I would like to sit in on your class today."

"Of course, Dr. Marcel. It would be an honor." Internally, I was screaming my head off. I had thirty minutes until the lecture, so I immediately headed across the quad to the library to fetch a coffee. Normally, I drank chai, but a strong black coffee was in order for today's impending fiasco. While waiting in line, I texted Sarah to let her know I was safe and sound.

Might even have a funny story for you next time we meet up, I added. She responded quickly — with a question mark.

"Here's your coffee." The frazzled student barista set it on the counter. She looked as if her morning had been even rougher than mine, which made me feel somewhat better. At least I wasn't still drunk, as I suspected of her.

I arrived in the lecture room relieved to find more than half of my students in attendance; that wasn't always the case on Fridays. A quick glance revealed Dr. Marcel in the back, along with William and Janice. Janice gave me a boisterous wave and a broad smile that suggested that no matter what I said she'd tell me I'd done a great job.

William, on the other hand, would not be so kind. His body language made it perfectly clear he intended to pounce on any mistake, no matter how slight.

I stifled a groan and waved at Dr. Marcel and Janice, resisting the urge to flip William the bird.

On the blackboard on the side of the stage, I wrote the word EQUALITY in capital letters. Generally, I tried not to write too much on the blackboard. My hands shook as a side effect of my Graves' disease, so my writing was almost always illegible to others. I'd become used to deciphering my chicken scratch out of necessity as a student. Focusing, I did my best to make the word large enough and clear enough for the people in the back row to see.

My watch beeped, alerting me that it was eight o'clock on the dot. "Good morning, everyone. Shall we begin?" I switched on the PowerPoint presentation by pressing a couple of buttons on the high-tech podium. "Today, we'll be discussing the French Revolution and the radical new term that emerged from this time period." I underlined the word on the board.

After a few moments, I forgot about the guests in the back row and fell into my normal lecturing groove. My queasiness subsided, as did the heaviness in my head. Standing in front of my students, giving a lecture, always gave me a natural high. Before I started teaching, I was so shy I never talked in class. But once I was on the opposite side of the lectern, I discovered my passion for teaching. Still, I couldn't deny that preparing for my lectures was the best part of my job. Research was in my blood.

When the quiet beep of my watch alerted me that I only had a few moments left before the end of class, I opened the floor to questions.

John, one of my brightest students, raised his hand.

"Yes, John."

"I'm just wondering, you said even those who believed in equality still tried to justify class differences ... I mean, even though they believed people should be equal, they didn't mean all across the board ... Was this the genesis of modern-day racism? Without degrees of equality, you can't have racism, right?" He leaned forward and rested his chin on his fist, resembling Rodin's statue *The Thinker*.

If it hadn't been completely inappropriate, I would have kissed John. "What a fantastic question! And very astute of you, I might add. On Monday, we'll be discussing *The Declaration of the Rights of Man* and paying particular attention to the first article. Then, together we can analyze John's question. Did everyone write that down?" There were some moans, but most of the students were too busy gathering their belongings to care. I sighed, but then forced a confident smile. They'd behaved pretty well for a Friday morning lecture, after all. "Have a great weekend."

I started to collect my notes from the podium.

Angela, the annoying eager beaver, who approached me after every class, pirouetted through the exiting students. Her shiny, perfect hair and unctuous smile grated on my nerves.

"Lizzie," she purred. I insisted all of my students call me by my first name.

I raised an eyebrow, doing my best to feign interest. It was obvious she was off her game today and couldn't think of anything clever to say. "Big plans this weekend?" I asked. I glanced over her head and noticed Dr. Marcel gathering the troops. Did I manage to give a halfway decent lecture, or was I doomed? I pictured being lined up outside, blindfolded with a cigarette dangling from my mouth, as the order was given for William to raise his gun ...

Angela's giggle brought me back to reality. "Going to read *The Declaration of the Rights of Man,* of course."

It was hard not to laugh in her face. I was a serious student at her age, but never an outright brownnoser. I didn't have to be, but Angela was on the cusp of earning a C, even though she'd made it clear to me on more than one occasion she'd never received a grade lower than a B.

"Don't study too much. It's bad for your health."

Her pinched face was priceless as she tried to figure out what I really meant.

I smiled and she reciprocated.

"I hope you manage to squeeze some fun in this weekend, Angela."

Luckily she realized I was giving her the brush-off. She waved a cheery hand. "Toodles."

Still giddy from the lecture, I parroted Angela, much to her delight, giving her the impression we'd just bonded.

My three guests sauntered to the front. The scowl on William's face was the best news of the day so far. I hadn't screwed up, and Dr. Marcel's glowing countenance confirmed I had knocked it out of the park.

What a relief!

"Well done, Lizzie. Well done." Dr. Marcel patted my back. "How about I take the three of you to breakfast?"

Janice never refused a chance to socialize, even if it meant having breakfast with our elderly teacher. William nodded, although I got the sense he'd rather have a colonoscopy. And Dr. Marcel grinned in a way that made it clear we would be discussing and praising my lecture. Although I hated attention, I also secretly craved it, especially from Dr. Marcel who was more like a parent to me than my own mom and dad. And to be able to watch William squirm in his seat would make it even better. He had to know his turn would be coming soon. Dr. Marcel usually sat in one of our lectures once a semester, but this was the first time Janice and William had accompanied him. I hoped that meant I would be sitting in on William's class, waiting for my opportunity to pounce.

Maybe I should drink grappa the night before every lecture. I made a mental note to thank Sarah — maybe by licking grappa off her entire body.

WE SAT IN a diner across the street, and before I could take a bite of pancake, William said, "I read your article in the *Quarterly*, Lizzie."

I set my fork down so I wouldn't attempt to stab him in the hand knowing he was getting ready to rip my argument to pieces.

"Did you? I must apologize. I still haven't read yours from the previous issue."

Janice stifled a snicker. Dr. Marcel scooped up a massive bite of omelet, oblivious to the tension.

"I must say I'm shocked by your conclusion. That the Boy Scouts and the Hitler Youth both co-opted the Back-to-Nature movement for paramilitary gain. The Hitler Youth, I give you. But the Boy Scouts?" His thin lips curled slightly but still didn't expose his teeth. To this day I still hadn't seen his pearly whites, or were they gnarly gray? What would he do if I attempted to lift up one of his lips with my knife?

"Have you read any of their manuals?"

"Can't say that I have, but — "

"I've read them. Every single one. How do you describe a group that plays games such as cutting the enemy's telegraph wires? Is that not a form of military training?"

We went back and forth until William stabbed his fork in my direction. "I was a Cub Scout and take great offence to your comparison."

"You were a scout in England before World War I?" I asked.

Dr. Marcel laughed. "And here I thought you were decades younger than me William. I didn't know you were old enough to be my grandfather."

Janice tittered.

William cleared his throat. "My father knows the head of the Boy Scouts."

"Of the United States of America. I think you missed that I analyzed the *British* Boy Scouts from their founding in 1908 up until World War One." I almost added, "Willy Boy," but ignored the urge. "Do I need to tell you the dates of World War One? I'll give you a hint, it happened before World War Two, which is your specialty." I tapped my fingers on the tabletop.

A flash of anger lit up his face and eyes.

Janice nudged my foot under the table, and the victorious look on her face let me know I was her hero for the day.

"Does anyone need a refill?" The waiter hefted a pot of coffee.

"I do." Dr. Marcel motioned to his cup, as did Janice. When the waiter left, he said, "Raise your glasses so we can toast Lizzie on her excellent lecture."

Dr. Marcel and Janice clicked their mugs against my orange juice glass. William seethed.

Typically, when William's claws came out, I did my best to maintain some sort of professional composure, but this morning, I let my hair down, so to speak. And it felt great.

"DID YOU SURVIVE the day?" Sarah's voice was a blend of concerned and sexy.

I relaxed into my desk chair at home and gripped my cell phone between my shoulder and my ear. "I did. And actually I should thank you."

"For getting you drunk on a school night?"

"Yes. It relaxed me completely. My professor and colleagues sat in on my class. Sarah, I knocked it out of the park. I wish you could have seen me." I rapped on the table with my pen.

She laughed. "Who knew grappa was your drink?"

I laughed with her. "How about you? How was your day?"

"In-ter-est-ing," she said, splitting the word into pronounced syllables. She sighed dramatically.

"Everything okay?" I was genuinely concerned, which was out of the ordinary for me. Most of the time, I was accused of being overly self-involved.

"Yeah, everything's fine. No reason to worry." Her tone lacked confidence, which of course made me worry more.

In the background I could have sworn I heard a woman's voice say, "Sarah, I need you."

"Hey, Lizzie, can I call you back later tonight? Or will you be sleeping?"

"Either way, call me."

"Okay." The smile returned to her voice. "Talk later."

I couldn't stop my mind from racing. I knew she spent a lot of time with her mom, but the woman sounded much younger. Her mom hadn't said much in the car last night, but I was 98.55 percent sure it wasn't her mother's voice.

So who was it?

Around midnight, Sarah called back, sounding as though she'd just finished a triathlon.

"Sorry for calling so late, but I promised to get back to you," she said.

"No worries. I wish I was with you. I'd put you to bed. You sound exhausted," I said while I scrunched a pillow under my head.

She sighed contentedly. "That would be nice, but don't fret, I'm heading home now."

"Wait? Are you driving?" I bolted up in bed.

"Yes, but I'm using hands-free. I like that, though."

"Like what?"

"That you're worried about me." She sounded so much more relaxed, and I couldn't help grinning.

Finally, I said, "Stay on the phone with me until you get home. I don't want you falling asleep at the wheel."

"Okay, Mom," she said, but I was fairly confident she wasn't peeved.

"Tell me about your day."

"Where to begin? I woke up with a doozy of a headache. Why did you order so many grappas?"

"Me?"

Her giggling soothed me. "You aren't saying I did, are you? I'm a responsible high school teacher. I would never get plowed on a Thursday." She was enjoying herself.

"So, only PhD students do such a thing?" I played along, relieved that she wasn't mentioning Meg. I hoped that was the first and last time Sarah interacted with my ex.

"Seems that way. What other naughty things do you do?"

"Ah, I can't say over the phone. Top secret."

"Sounds promising." I heard her take a deep breath. "I'm home."

"Good. Now I'm ordering you straight to bed."

"Mine or yours?"

I paused, contemplating whether she would be too tired to come over.

"Don't worry, I was just kidding." My pause must have given her the wrong message.

"Too bad. I was trying to decide whether you were too tired or not."

"Really?" She sounded pleasantly shocked. "Maybe we

should wait."

I almost blurted out, "Hopefully not too long," but instead said, "Good night, Sarah. Have sweet dreams."

"I will now."

I closed my eyes and imagined Sarah's naked body pressed against mine. My hand slipped into my panties. This was quickly becoming a nightly ritual, and I hoped the real Sarah would be joining me in bed, not just the fantasy.

Chapter Six

"Why, Lizzie, you sound smitten." Ethan batted his eyelashes at me.

"Smitten? Please. People like me don't fall in love." I waved him off.

"Interesting. I didn't mention the L-word." Ethan's curious expression unnerved me, or maybe he was hitting too close to home for my liking.

I rolled my eyes. "I just find her fascinating really. I mean, I'm no Don Juan, but she finds my clumsy attempts to woo her charming. For the life of me, I can't figure out why."

He laughed. "Stop trying to figure everything out. You'll drive yourself crazy. Just relax and enjoy."

Two concepts I wasn't familiar with. "But what happens when – ?"

He put a palm in the air. "Good Lord! You could talk yourself out of a free cheese sample at a farmer's market."

"Free cheese? Why would I turn down free cheese? Is it not sanitary? No toothpicks?"

Ethan shook his head as if he was trying to determine whether I was a Martian. "What's wrong with you?"

I slapped the table. "That's what I'm telling you! What

happens when Sarah looks at me like you're doing now?" I frantically circled my finger in front of his face.

He attempted to swipe his confusion away with his palm. It didn't work. "Just be yourself. So far it's working for you."

I nodded, even though I could detect a hint of caution in his tone. Be myself. I could try that for a bit. First time for everything. At first, with Meg it was easier, since she expected me to be a scholar first and foremost. And she was all about Meg. When things got bad, I spent more time concentrating on every word I uttered since Meg had become a pro at twisting everything and turning innocent words into an insult. Once, during a cold snap, I mentioned her lips were so blue she looked like a Smurf. Meg pounced and said I was making a dig about needing to drink to cope with her depression. To this day, I still can't wrap my head around that one.

Sarah was much less threatening, but I had a feeling she wanted to get to know the real me. Delve into my deepest desires, wants, needs, and fears — that thought stopped me dead.

Ethan leaned closer. "My advice is hold onto her. You won't find many who find such a clueless person endearing." He hooted.

"Thanks, buddy. *You* don't mind my company."

"True, true. Somehow I manage to make it through our weekly chats." He kicked my foot and grinned. Then he took a sip of coffee. "How are your seminars going?"

"Good, except for William."

"He still gunning for you?" He mimicked firing a gun with both hands, adding machine-gun noises.

"Every chance he gets. I swear that guy won't stop trying to destroy me until he's dead. Last week he attempted to tear apart my journal article in the *European History Quarterly*."

"You've definitely made an enemy of him."

"I didn't do anything!"

Ethan chuckled. "You sounded just like a squirrel. William will never accept that Dr. Marcel chose you over him. I'm sure he's convinced you used nefarious tricks, maybe even sex."

Why did everyone insert sex or sexual references into everything lately? It was tiresome. No wonder I preferred books.

I crinkled my nose, ignoring the last statement. "Nefarious tricks. I've published and co-written twice the amount of articles he has since we started our program."

"He doesn't see it that way. He's a Thornhill, and Thornhills always get their way. It was probably the first time he'd failed."

"Second."

Ethan quirked an eyebrow.

"Janice found out he wasn't accepted into Oxford's program."

"Really?" Ethan's pitch spiked to a near operatic level. "I remember when he introduced himself to me years ago, before I could say my name he had explained why he was in Fort Collins for school."

"Dr. Marcel?"

"You got it." He tilted his cup in my direction.

Dr. Marcel used to teach at Harvard. He was one of the top professors in the field, if not the top. However, his wife grew tired of Massachusetts' brutal winters and sweltering summer humidity, so they moved here. It was quite the coup for our school.

"I got the same spiel. He tells it to everyone. I've wondered if he has it recorded on his phone so he doesn't have to waste a breath on low-life academics like us. It's hard to tell whether he's actually talking." I mimicked the weird thing William did with his lips.

Ethan burst into laughter. "Every time I spoke with him, I used to watch his lips. I never saw them moving. Not once! Does he have teeth?"

"It must be exhausting expending so much energy to look like one isn't expending any."

Ethan shrugged. "I don't think it's much fun being William."

"Probably not. It's not much fun being the one he's always gunning for, either."

"Be careful. He's the type who'll shoot you in the back."

"At least I'll get a couple of weeks of peace and quiet soon during our research break — the best part of grad school. No classes so we can focus on our semester research projects."

Ethan leaned back in his chair. "I do miss it. While you'll be in hog heaven, my in-laws are coming." His pained expression made me laugh.

"Not looking forward to it?" I teased.

He shook his head. "Relationships do have some downsides: in-laws being at the top of most people's lists. When are you going to introduce Sarah to the fam? It's so much fun." He let out a fake squeal and clapped his hands together.

"Ha! It worked so well last time."

He tutted. "Well, the relationship is still new, so probably best not to make plans." He knew full well the idea hadn't crossed my mind.

I thought of Meg and how she'd used her knowledge of my family, especially the money, against me. Not that Ethan knew that.

As if in tune with my thoughts, he smiled. "It might be a bit early to show Sarah where you came from. Don't half of the Denver Broncos live in your neighborhood?"

I shrugged. "And a few hockey players."

"Any movie stars?"

"Nah. I think they have vacation homes in Aspen, not on the outskirts of Denver."

"You and William have a lot more in common than you like to think."

"Am I as much of an asshole?"

"It depends on the day." He winked to soften the blow.

It didn't.

Chapter Seven

IT WAS A RELIEF WHEN the research break ended. Usually, I loved my alone time and used it to concentrate on the nitty-gritty aspects of my dissertation, but this time being away from everyone and everything had been lonelier than normal.

To make matters worse, I didn't see Sarah once. We spoke on the phone most days, but I swear her calendar was fuller than the president's. If she wasn't coaching or attending meetings, she was tutoring underprivileged kids or stepping in as the faculty member for the school's gay group. Her latest kick was volunteering at a food bank with some of her high school students. And it wasn't like I could make a stink about that. I loved Sarah's drive, but shit, where did I fit in?

I closed my eyes and pretended I was sitting on the couch with Sarah, nestling my head on her shoulder. Her intoxicating jasmine perfume filled my nostrils.

An annoying voice ended the daydream.

"All she did was party and eat." William flipped through the pages of his copy of *Berlin Diaries* by Marie Vassiltchikov. It was Tuesday evening, and I was sitting in my Daily Life in World War II reading seminar. "I don't see the merit in reading this." William hardly ever saw the merit of any book we read. This was one of the negative aspects of academia. Everyone wanted to "uncover" a diary, letter, or any type of evidence to shed new light on subjects that had been put through the scholarly wringer. So when something new came out, most academics jumped all over the author because more than likely it'd refute their own theories. I wished one of Dr. Marcel's books was on the list to see if he had the balls to tear into it per usual.

Dr. Marcel shifted in his seat, smiling but not yet ready to speak.

I twisted back to William. "How would you survive the war?"

"You think she was partying to survive?" William tsked skeptically. "She was a spoiled brat."

Takes one to know one, I thought. "I do. She was a white Russian living in Berlin under the Nazis. It wasn't like she had a lot of options. She couldn't go back to the Soviet Union because the Reds were in charge and she was an aristocrat. Due to her background, she knew a lot of wealthy and important people in Germany, so naturally she went to their gatherings and parties. She used that to her advantage. There were bombings, firestorms, and food shortages. Considering what methods others took, I don't understand your vitriol against her." I stopped, but then another thought struck me. "And she was working for the resistance and knew about — or maybe was involved in — the plot to assassinate Hitler. Would you have the guts to do that, William?"

He gawped at me, and then his eyes narrowed. "Oh, please." He waved a dismissive hand. "She cared more about name-dropping than about killing Hitler. This book is all about her."

I shook both hands in the air, imagining wringing his skinny neck. "It's her diary!"

"I think Lizzie's onto something," Janice said in a calm tone. "At first, I got tired of her name-dropping, but then I started to put the pieces together. Even if you don't like her, you have to admit she provided a wonderful glimpse into civilian life in Berlin during the war." Janice was the only other student in the seminar. If it weren't for William, the vibe would have been cozy and educational rather than confrontational. William was dead set on holding the opposite opinion to me. If we'd discussed *Mein Kampf*, would he insist it was wonderful and well written since I would be the one tearing it to shreds? I kept hearing Ethan's machine-gun sounds in my head.

William snorted. "You're just as bad as Lizzie — so practical you think everyone else is practical."

Janice and I exchanged an amused smile.

"What do you mean?" I asked.

William placed a palm on the table. "What I mean, Lizzie, is that you don't have any human emotions. You think like a robot, and you think everyone else is as logical as you. Do you remember our movie conversation?"

Janice bristled for me. "Something tells me you're mad about another thing, Willy Boy." She pinned him with a glare and jerked her head in Dr. Marcel's direction. Janice had also applied to work with our professor. Unlike William, she didn't hold any grudges.

"Are you talking about *Casablanca* ... weeks ago?" I asked, stunned.

Why was he still thinking about that? I knew he considered himself a lot like Bogie. Had he taken it as a personal slight? I'd only stated what I would have done, speaking theoretically and pragmatically. Sometimes it was hard not to think like a historian. Hindsight's twenty-twenty.

"We all know why you're opposed to love, don't we?" William sneered.

Even though I tried to keep the tittle-tattle about my relationship with Meg to a minimum on campus, college campuses were rife with gossip and backstabbing. After the breakup, Meg had been forced out of the program. Soon after, she'd entered rehab. She'd never outright blamed me, but she'd never come to my defense either. Me, I stayed mute on the subject, which only made it look worse. No one except Janice knew how hard I'd tried to keep Meg off booze. No one knew about all the nights I'd held her and all the times I'd copped her abuse. Meg was a mess. I'd done everything I could, including getting her into rehab and paying for it, but I could never tell others what it was like behind the scenes, both out of respect for Meg and, truth be told, also out of embarrassment. What I'd put up with made my skin crawl, even today.

"You just love ruining academic careers, don't you?" William continued.

"That's enough!" Janice's glare suggested she wanted to rip his head off and shove it down his puckered mouth. "I'm so tired of your whining. You think Vassiltchikov was bad. You've been moping ever since Dr. Marcel made his choice. Get over it. If you can't, get out. In every discussion you try to humiliate Lizzie. It's time to let it go. It's been over two years. Get the fuck over it!" She slapped the table.

I pivoted to Janice, my mouth hanging open. She was usually so laid-back, not the type to throw down the gauntlet. Her face was beet-red, and she inhaled deeply, trying to regain her composure.

Our usually silent professor let out a puff of air as he drummed two fingers against his lips. His teaching method involved getting the ball rolling during the first few minutes of class and then sitting back to let us work our way through the discussion. Half the time we bickered about what we thought was relevant or pure drivel.

William's eyes burned with rage. "I don't know what you're

talking about. I'm trying to engage you two in dialogue." By the end of the sentence, his voice was barely a whisper.

Dr. Marcel cleared his throat. "I think that's enough for this evening."

Janice stormed out of the room. As I packed my books and notebook into my bag, Dr. Marcel said, "William, do you have time to talk?"

I didn't have to study William's face to sense his resolve wilting.

"Yes. Of course, sir."

I left the room silently, without my usual adieu to Dr. Marcel.

Janice stood outside, opening a pack of cigarettes. She wiggled the box, asking if I wanted one.

I shook my head. "No thanks. I don't smoke." Janice, of course, knew that.

She lit hers and took a long, angry drag. "He's such a fuckstick."

"Has been from day one," I said. "Dr. Marcel is talking to him now, I think."

She blew a puff of smoke out her nostrils. "Really! About time. Don't let him get to you. I was friends with you and Meg." She studied me cautiously, knowing the topic made me uncomfortable. "I know you did everything you could for her."

Avoiding her gaze, I responded with a non-committal shrug.

"Have you seen her lately?" Janice flicked her cigarette.

"Just last week, unfortunately." I focused on the ash floating in the air, thinking of all the money I'd given to Meg disappearing into a black hole.

"I saw her yesterday. Not a fan of the red hair, and what's up with the black fingernail polish?" She took another hit, released the smoke, and said, "Looks like a prossie."

"Prossie?"

"You need a one-a-day calendar from the *Urban Dictionary*. Prostitute."

My opinion of Meg wasn't very high, but prostitute? No way. My belly growled, causing both of us to laugh.

"Do you have plans for dinner?" I asked.

She noted the time on her watch and then dropped her cigarette on the ground and pulverized it with her shoe. "Shit! Collin's in town, and I'm late for our date." She laughed and then sang, "I'm late for a *very* important date," and scurried away, reminiscent of the white rabbit from *Alice in Wonderland*. It was a relief to see her back to her normal self.

William stormed out of the glass doors, saw me, paused, and then waltzed off in the opposite direction, holding his torso ramrod straight instead of his typical end of day slouch.

Sighing, I walked to the bike rack and freed my Cannondale. It was a cold night, and for the first time in a long time I wished I'd driven my car that morning. I briefly wondered whether Sarah would come and get me, but the fear of her being with someone else held me back. Lately, every time I called, I got the impression she wasn't alone. There weren't any more voices in the background, but intuition told me to be wary. I sensed Sarah was being overly cautious about what she said and how she acted. Like she wasn't alone. I wasn't sure what to think about that. Besides, she was still having issues with her car.

"Get moving and stop feeling sorry for yourself," I snapped.

Chapter Eight

"WAIT, ARE YOU TELLING ME you would rather be with the other guy than Humphrey Bogart?" Ethan covered his mouth with a palm as though he was trying to trap more shocked words inside.

The altercation with William still rankled. Stupidly I'd brought it up during our coffee date. Ethan honed in on the *Casablanca* part, not the Meg aspect, which was a relief, to some degree.

"And stay in Casablanca and be with a guy who owned a bar that's controlled by the Vichy and swarming with Nazis and Italian fascists? Are you kidding me?" I crossed my arms.

"What about love?" Ethan said.

"What about surviving?"

"What's the point of living without love?"

I sighed.

Ethan's smirk widened. "You know, you're Sally."

Sally?

What was he talking about? I motioned for him to fill me in, too exasperated to verbalize it.

"*When Harry Met Sally.*"

"Who are Harry and Sally?" I crinkled my nose as if Harry and Sally had body odor.

Ethan rolled his eyes so hard I thought they might roll right out of his head. "Seriously? You haven't seen that movie?"

"Is it a new release?"

"Uh, no. It's a classic."

"What year? I love classics." I sat up straight in my seat, like I did in class.

Ethan rubbed his chin. "I don't know. The eighties."

I laughed. "The eighties. That doesn't count as a classic! Sorry."

He waved his hand, dismissing me. "In the movie, Harry and Sally get into a discussion about *Casablanca*, and Meg Ryan, who plays Sally, says she would rather leave with the other guy instead of staying in Casablanca with the guy who owns a bar. She claims women are more practical than that."

"I'm not getting your point."

"You have to see the movie to get the counterargument."

I let out a huff of angry air. "Can't you just fill me in?"

"Okay, but you may not like it."

"Try me." I waved him on.

"Billy Crystal's character — he plays Harry — says he understands and his theory is ... that Sally hasn't had great sex."

"And?"

"And what?"

I slapped the tabletop. "What does that mean?"

"Sex? Geez, do I need to get out the dolls or something?"

I shook my head angrily. "How does that apply to me?" I enunciated each word carefully.

"You really are clueless about some things, aren't you? I'm just saying you should be careful telling people you'd leave Humphrey Bogart in the dust for a passionless marriage. People might think you're more frigid than you really are."

"They'll think I'm a Sally." Realization slowly seeped in.

Oddly, Ethan was way more comfortable talking about sex than I was. It seemed everyone was lately. Or maybe I was just noticing it more since meeting Sarah. I was pretty good about tuning people out when they ventured into topics I'd prefer to leave unsaid. Since Sarah, though, everything was reminding me of intimacy, and I'd been entertaining way more sexual fantasies than I ever had with Meg.

"Exactly! Most people our age have probably seen *When Harry Met Sally*. Not sure about *Casablanca*."

"Oh, come on. *Casablanca* is a classic!"

"It is. How many times have you seen it?"

"I don't know, half a dozen or more. I own the DVD."

Ethan eyeballed me. "Interesting. And each time you think she should leave?"

I nodded without any hesitation.

"Good Lord. That makes me worry about you."

"Why?" I raised my shoulders.

"I don't know how to explain it. How do you explain love to someone who doesn't feel love?"

"Doesn't feel love." I scoffed. "I understand love."

"Understand?" he asked.

I curled my lips. "What do you know anyway? Need I remind you that just the thought of sex and all the fluids makes you cringe?"

He jutted his chin before waving my diversionary tactic to the side. Damn.

"How did you feel about Meg?" He leaned in.

"Let's not talk about her, okay? Look how that ended." I pushed my chair back.

He nodded knowingly. "So, you would rather steer clear of love to avoid getting your heart trampled on again."

"I'm not avoiding love."

"When's the last time you saw Sarah?"

I paused and ran a mental check through my calendar. "Uh, last week, briefly." It was longer than that.

"I thought you liked her."

"I do."

"But not enough to pursue?" He turned his head to the side.

"What? No," I said too quickly. I was embarrassed to admit that Sarah was the one who was playing hard to get, not me. When we talked, everything seemed okay, but getting her schedule to match mine was almost as complicated as cracking the German code during World War II. "I like Sarah, I do. She's beautiful, smart, funny, and caring."

"But?"

"I think she's seeing someone else." The sentence slipped out.

"What?" Ethan's brow furrowed.

"Once when we spoke on the phone, a woman in the background said, 'Sarah, I need you,' and it was a young voice, not her mother's."

"Her mother?" He looked confused.

"She and her mom are really close." I raised my hands, indicating go figure.

"Don't read too much into what you heard. Just because she was with another woman doesn't mean they're dating. Normal people have friends." He stressed the last sentence for me.

I ignored his comment about normal people. "What if, though? We only see each other occasionally. For all I know, she could be dating tons of women."

Ethan ignored my comment and placed his hand on my arm. "Let it happen. Call her. Don't let that mind of yours ruin something before it has a chance to really start."

I had been calling her. And texting. All to no avail. Of course I would never tell Ethan that. That was why I avoided getting close to people. It opened me up to feeling like there was something missing when the other person was absent. I hated that feeling. It made me lonelier than when I was alone.

LATER THAT AFTERNOON, I sat at my desk in my apartment with my cell phone in front of me and contemplated Ethan's advice. Should I call Sarah and insist on a date? Okay, maybe not *insist*, but ask. Plead? Get down on my hands and knees?

Each time I reached for the phone, I stopped.

"This is bloody ridiculous," I muttered to myself. "Just call her."

Still I hesitated.

I decided to flip a coin. Heads I would. Tails I wouldn't.

It came up tails.

So I called her. Screw the damn coin.

"Lizzie, it's so good to hear your voice." Her welcoming tone put me at ease right away. "How've you been?"

"Same old, same old," I said as breezily as possible. "The life of a grad student is so exciting. Sleep, study, sleep, study."

"What about eating?"

"I do occasionally." I laughed, thinking of the many sandwiches I consumed daily.

"You need someone to take care of you. How about we grab dinner later this week?" She paused.

I gathered she was checking her calendar, and I tried to block out the fictitious female names that appeared on each day. "Would Friday work? Just in case we get drunk?" She giggled.

"Sounds great. See ya Friday."

"That, you can count on." Her voice implied "and then some," and a pulsing I hadn't felt in a long time stirred through my body. I set my phone down and inhaled and exhaled several times to steady my whizzing throb.

Chapter Nine

ON FRIDAY AFTERNOON, I RECEIVED a text from Sarah: *I'm beat. Can we do takeout and a movie at your place instead?*

I was surprised she still wanted to see me if she was that exhausted, but I wasn't going to argue. I missed her. That thought alone made me shake my head. If Ethan knew, he'd be fluttering his eyelids and saying some cockamamie thing about being smitten.

Around six, I heard a soft knock on my front door, and my skin sizzled as if I'd just fallen into a geyser at Yellowstone. Was that what love felt like: hot, beyond painful, and terrifying?

"Can you believe this weather?" Sarah kissed me on the cheek and walked in.

I stuck my head out the door. The rain was now a slushy snow. Within a few hours the roads wouldn't be drivable, the moisture on them freezing under the snow.

"Huh, hard to believe. It was sunny a few hours ago." I watched the snow fall until I remembered that Sarah was standing right behind me, upon which I slammed the door shut immediately, as if afraid she'd dash out of the place in protest at my rudeness. "Here, let me take your coat."

She spun around and I eased it over her shoulders. "Would

you like some tea or hot chocolate to warm up?"

Her nose resembled a red button on a snowman.

"Yes, please. Hot chocolate." She rubbed her hands together. "I had to park over in the next lot. It seems everyone is tucked in for the weekend."

"Did you get a new car?"

"I borrowed my mom's." She avoided my eyes. Was she embarrassed about her car woes?

"I ordered pizza, but maybe I should order Chinese or something for the rest of the weekend."

"Yes. Or we'll starve!"

I eyed her questioningly, until I realized I'd said the Chinese bit out loud. I hadn't been thinking about the two of us. Then it dawned on me – the storm meant it would be safer for her to stay the night. From the increasing size of the flakes, Sarah might be here all weekend. I smiled foolishly.

"Okay. Let's go to the kitchen, get your hot chocolate going, and find some takeout menus to peruse."

She nodded and led the way to the kitchen. I barely remembered the night she'd practically carried me in here after the grappa incident, but her recollection seemed much clearer.

Soon the kettle whistled. Sarah leaned against the counter, examining a Chinese menu as if her life depended on it. It might. Before she glommed on to the menus she'd inspected my fridge and cupboards and found them entirely lacking, except for sandwich ingredients, hummus, and fruit.

"Do you only eat sandwiches?" she asked, still studying the menu.

"Or takeout."

She extracted her cell phone from the back pocket of her jeans and dialed. "Yes, I'd like to place an order ... for takeout ... oh, how much? Okay." She rolled her eyes at me and then rattled off my address. I was amazed she had it memorized. She ordered more food than I would have; it would take us days to eat it all.

I tried to stop my eyes from widening at her list of dishes, worrying I would get a headache from the strain.

"Wow! I'm putting you in charge of ordering from now on," I said when she ended the call. "It might be easier next time if you say *the entire menu, please*."

She laughed. "I know you can eat. Better to be safe than sorry. And it's my favorite takeout place in town. Can you believe they're charging a fee for delivering in a blizzard? He said ours was the last order they were accepting. Apparently the roads will be closed by nine."

"Blizzard? Is it going to be that bad?"

Sarah whacked my arm. "Don't you follow The Weather Channel? They say we're expecting two feet."

"Why would I follow The Weather Channel?" I handed her a steaming mug of hot chocolate. Each day I peeked outside and assessed the weather. Of course, Colorado's weather was fickle. The saying was: don't like the weather, wait ten minutes and it'll change. So why bother following it when conditions would invariably change anyway?

Sarah didn't bother to answer. Instead, she bolted for the front room, responding to a faint knock on the door. "How did they get here so fast?" she asked.

"I think it's the pizza I ordered." I tried to hide a smile.

She smacked her forehead.

Sure enough it was. A boy barely old enough to shave stood on my front stoop with three large pizza boxes and several smaller containers of chicken wings, garlic bread, and cinnamon treats. "Forty-one bucks." He sounded pissed.

I gave him fifty. "Keep the change."

A brief smile crossed his face, but he sighed as he turned

back to the near whiteout conditions. No wonder the Chinese place was charging extra. Capitalism at its best.

"And you said I ordered a lot." Sarah took the containers off the top of the pizza boxes, allowing me to see. "What did you get?"

Without waiting for a reply, she headed back to the kitchen. "Good thing your fridge is nearly empty; we'll have room to store all this."

"And you have to stay until it's gone." I had no clue why that slipped out, but I immediately felt like an idiot for saying it. Usually, I liked my alone time. But the longing in Sarah's eyes pushed those thoughts out of my mind making it clear that my head wasn't in control tonight.

"That sounds nice. I've missed you." Without further ado, she flipped open the boxes.

I handed her a plate, watching in amazement as she stacked four slices on it. "And I thought *I* ate a lot," I said.

She grinned guiltily. "I haven't eaten much this week, what with work and ..." She avoided my gaze and didn't finish.

"Are you okay?"

Her eyes glistened with tears. "It's been a rough week."

I encircled her in my arms, and she rested her head on my shoulder. "You don't have to talk, but I'm here."

Her arms tightened around my waist, but she didn't try to speak, and I didn't force her to. We had all weekend, hopefully. Besides, I wasn't the type to pry.

After we carried our plates to the front room, Sarah powered up the stereo and dug some CDs from her purse. "I hope you don't mind, but I'm not in the mood for audiobooks." She winked.

"I won't give up, you know. I'll convert you yet."

Taking the CDs from her, I selected one at random. There wasn't any indication of the band name, just a date: May 10, 2011.

I took that as a promising sign. What can I say? I was that much of a history nerd.

We settled on the couch, and I chomped into a slice of cheese pizza. Sarah regarded her plate with disinterest, as if her appetite had slipped away from the sand like a wave returning to the ocean. I set my slice down and took her hand in mine. "Talk to me. What's wrong?"

A floodgate opened, wetting her cheeks, but after a while she sucked in air and sobbed. "I'm sorry. It's just been a horrendous week. One of my students tried to kill herself."

I hugged her, unsure what to say — if anything.

"We're trained to see the signs, but no one noticed a thing. And I'm really close to her. I feel like such a failure." We both sank back into the couch where I rocked her gently, completely at a loss. Sarah didn't seem to mind. She held me back, tightly, and then, moments later, leaned away and wiped her eyes with a paper napkin.

"Do you want something to drink?" I asked lamely. "Something stronger than hot chocolate?"

Her eyes brightened. "Oh, I picked up some wine. And rum and Coke for you." She reached for her handbag, which was more like a piece of luggage, and hauled out the loot. "What do you say? Will you get drunk with me?"

"How can I refuse?" I said, rising to get some glasses.

"I'm surprised you actually have wineglasses," she said, when I returned from the kitchen holding a wineglass and my concoction. The look that flashed across her pretty face made my pulse quicken.

"I'm not a complete Neanderthal. I just don't cook." I picked up one of the bottles. "I even know how to use one of these." I held up my corkscrew.

"Knowing how to screw is important."

I flashed her my I-can't-believe-you-just-said-that smile.

She saluted with her wineglass as a thank-you. "This will help me some, but tell me what's new with you to get my mind off things."

"Have you seen the movie *Casablanca*?" I asked.

She scrunched her forehead. "Yeah, why?"

I told her about my confrontation with William. It paled in comparison to her story, but it was all I had, and I was feeling put on the spot. Since Meg, my life had been uncomplicated — just the way I wanted it to be. Or so I'd thought.

"Seriously? You wouldn't stay with Humphrey Bogart?" she asked.

I kicked myself for entering the *Casablanca* fray yet again.

"Don't say it." I put up my palm for emphasis.

Sarah cocked her head. "Say what?"

"Don't call me a Sally?"

She laughed. "A Sally? What are you talking about?"

I studied her face to see if she was holding back. "So, you haven't seen it either?" I shook my head, victorious. Ethan didn't know jack shit.

She placed a hand on my thigh. "What in the world are you going on about?"

"*When Harry Met Sally*," I said in all seriousness.

"Of course I saw *that*. Years ago, but what does this have to do — ?"

It was as if I could see the thought invade her mind. She covered her mouth in a weak attempt to suppress laughter.

"Did William call you a Sally?"

I blanched at the thought. "No, thank God. Ethan did, when we had coffee last week. Now my best friend and my colleagues think I've never had great sex." In the beginning, sex with Meg was satisfying. It wasn't until her drinking became uncontrollable that every relationship aspect besides caregiver was left in the dust.

"Colleagues. You talk about your sex life with colleagues?" Her sour expression screamed *danger*!

"No," I waved both hands in the air. "The conversation got out of hand, but I nipped it in the bud. I don't even discuss it much with Ethan, my best friend."

"Is Ethan the one who ...?" She seemed unsure how to continue.

"Yes. He's the one who can't stand bodily fluids."

For some reason that made her laugh. "And he thinks you aren't good in bed. Oh, that's rich."

"Hey now. Don't put those thoughts in my head."

She kissed my cheek, taking me by surprise. "Wait ... you haven't seen *When Harry Met Sally?*"

Taken aback that she'd disengaged to ask me about a silly movie from the eighties, I shook my head.

"Next time, we have to watch it."

"We can tonight. I picked up a copy to figure out what Ethan was talking about."

Sarah squealed with delight. I had high hopes she would squeal much more later, but I knew I had to go slow. She was still not her normal bubbly self.

"You know, ever since the first time I met you, I thought you were a bit clueless."

Clueless? Was she trying to compliment me?

"Uh ..."

"Don't worry. I think it's endearing."

That relieved me a little.

"And then there's that smile of yours."

"What smile?" I knew I was smiling, but I couldn't help it.

"That one!" She placed a hand on my cheek. "I love that smile."

An uncomfortable silence hung between us.

I sipped my rum and Coke, while Sarah stared at my bookshelf across the room. Finally, she asked shyly, "What's your dissertation on?"

I paused, taken aback by the abrupt change of subject. "The Hitler Youth."

"The what?"

"The Hitler Youth. Nazis' version of the Boy Scouts."

"Oh, that explains it."

"Explains what?"

"Why you have so many books with swastikas on the covers." She waved at my bookshelves. "I have to admit, it's off-putting at first. I wasn't sure about you when I strolled in that first night."

"Ah." I refilled her glass. "Before I invite another woman over, I'll need to do a de-Nazification sweep of my apartment." I laughed; she didn't.

Her pinched face and tense shoulders told me I had screwed up again — or was she thinking of her student? Dating was a minefield. Afraid to ask what she was thinking, I thought over what I'd just said, hearing my own words again and understanding how she might have taken them. No wonder I was single. I lacked charm, conversational skills, and panache. A rattlesnake probably had more dating smarts. Was there a Dummy's guide for surviving dating?

Sarah must have felt sorry for me, because she asked, "How many women have you had since the big breakup?"

"Big breakup?"

"Just a guess, but I think I'm right, considering you're hedging." She winked.

I spoke into my glass. "None."

"Was it that woman from the Italian place?"

I squirmed in my seat, neither confirming nor denying.

"How long ago did the relationship end?" she asked.

"Over a year."

"And you haven't had …?"

I had to laugh. "You're inquisitive … and feisty. I like that about you."

That softened her up a little.

"What else do you like?" she asked.

Oh, God. I was going to have to try to stay one step ahead of her, or she'd eat me alive. "Ha! Smooth!" I leaned over, one inch from her face. "You're beautiful, intelligent, and you have extremely soft lips."

She didn't pull away. "How do you know? About the lips part? We haven't kissed."

Our mouths were almost close enough to smooch. I hesitated. Sarah beamed, daring me. I went for it. Her lips were soft and moist, and I could taste the wine on her tongue.

The doorbell rang and I broke away awkwardly. "The Chinese is here," I said. "I mean, the food is here."

The odd expression in her eyes made it hard for me to determine whether she was impressed by our kiss; I was, but I sensed my opinion didn't really matter. In this instance, only Sarah mattered.

During the transaction at the door, Sarah stood right behind me, so close I could feel her body heat. It was exhilarating.

"Thanks, lady!" the young man said when I told him to keep the change. Math wasn't my strong suit, so I always erred on the side of caution.

"What do you say? Shall we skip the pizza, since it's probably cold by now?" I said.

She nodded enthusiastically. I had to admit the aroma of the Chinese food was making my stomach cartwheel in anticipation.

"Pizza is perfect for breakfast," Sarah said as I directed her to the dining room.

"Would you like some silverware?" I asked, setting chopsticks next to my place setting; I'd prepared the table for us both earlier, even if only for pizza.

"Wait, are you going to use chopsticks?" She placed her hands on her hips.

I struggled to interpret her body language. "Uh, yeah. Unless you would prefer I use Western silverware."

"Western silverware!" She let out a snort of laughter. "Do you always talk like that?"

"Like what?"

"A teacher."

"I am a teacher."

The most beautiful grin spread across her face. God, did she know how sexy she was?

"Besides, you're a teacher," I pointed out, needlessly. Of course she knew she was a teacher. That was how we'd met, after all.

Sarah tipped her head in agreement. "I'm just impressed; that's all." She took her seat. "I've been on dates with people who wouldn't even try using chopsticks in a Chinese restaurant, and here you are using them in your own home."

I mentally ticked another point in my favor and then motioned for her to dig in.

"So, did you rush home and clean this place after my text?" She placed a linen napkin in her lap.

Shaking my head, I replied, "Nope. Why? Is it a mess?" I dished out egg-fried rice.

"Your apartment is always this clean?" Her eyes bulged as she took in the room. "There's not a speck of dust, and the surfaces in your kitchen have a Mr. Clean shine."

"Oh, that. I'm a bit of a neat freak." I laughed nervously. "I can't take the credit. Miranda" — I noticed her eyebrows join in confusion — "my cleaner does all the work a few times a week," I added hastily.

"You have a housecleaner?" She didn't try to hide the incredulous inflection in her tone.

"Uh, yeah." I shrugged. "Is that bad?"

Sarah shook her head. "No. But I haven't met anyone our age who does."

"I pay her well." I defended myself like a total moron.

She laughed. "I'm sure you do. I'm just surprised; that's all. No judgment, I promise." She crossed her heart before picking up her chopsticks and dipping into the orange beef.

"I love your rustic dining table and chairs. I'm betting you didn't get this at American Furniture." I shook my head. "Next time I'll bring a flower centerpiece. Oak?" She rapped her knuckles on the table.

"Russian oak," I scooped out a heaped portion of sesame chicken, enough to feed two people, maybe three. Sarah peered over the table at my overloaded plate.

"Sorry, I have Graves' disease." I motioned with my chopsticks to all the food and then rubbed my thyroid with my left hand, a habit that was hard to break when the subject surfaced.

"Oh ..."

"It's nothing to be alarmed about, really. It just means I have a hyperactive thyroid, so my appetite is always out of control. I take pills," I explained, neglecting to tell her that I took them to stay alive; that freaked some people out. It had freaked me out when my doctor instructed me to go straight to the pharmacy and get my prescription filled after he'd broken the news. "That's why I'm relieved you ordered enough for four. I didn't want you to starve."

"I thought you just didn't want to share," she teased, relaxing into her seat. She bit into an egg roll and licked a crumb off her lip.

I wanted her tongue on me. I shifted in my seat, trying to ignore the warm sensation between my legs.

"Oh, don't worry, I'll probably dip into yours." I instantly regretted my word choice. I wasn't even going for a double entendre.

"I hope so." She didn't bother to play coy.

After the whole Meg debacle, I hadn't thought I'd ever want to be with a woman again. With my career, I thought I could stay busy and be reasonably happy and satisfied. Women were nothing but an emotional drain, I convinced myself, not that I'd had much experience besides Meg. The short flings during my undergrad days didn't count. But sitting across from Sarah, in my own home, I felt complete. *Not that I'm pursuing a serious relationship*, I chastised myself. Commitment wasn't on the to-do list.

"Tell me about your family," she said without any trace of malice. Not that there was usually any malice in the question; it was a perfectly normal question. Problem was I didn't have a normal family, and I couldn't think of them without malice.

"I have an older brother who lives in California. My parents live in Denver." I hoped she hadn't noticed I gave the barest of details.

"Are you close?"

I cleared my throat, unsure how to proceed. "Not really. How about you?"

"I'm an only child, and my father died when I was quite young."

I reached across and squeezed her hand. "I'm so sorry."

She squeezed back, holding onto my fingertips for a few seconds. The heat from her hand sparked sensations I hadn't felt in some time. Was it wrong that I was picturing her naked right after she'd told me her father was dead?

"I don't remember him really. Mom and I are very close. We go shopping together every Saturday."

"Every Saturday?" I choked on some fried rice and then guzzled rum and Coke to ease my blocked airway.

"You don't like to shop?" She smiled, considering my reaction.

I shook my head. "I even have my groceries delivered."

"You eat in the dining room, have a housecleaner, and have your groceries delivered. Where are you hiding Jeeves?" she joked. At least I think she was kidding.

"I gave him the night off."

She guffawed, and we ate in companionable silence for a few moments.

"Do you feel weird being surrounded by swastikas?" She pointed her chopsticks to a stack of books behind me.

"I guess I don't notice it. I've been studying Nazis so long I'm just used to it."

She scrunched up her face.

"Not that I am one, of course. I mean … I'm fascinated. When I started researching the Hitler Youth and the indoctrination of millions of children … well, it astounded me. Still does, even after all this time. I'm lucky … most grad students are sick and tired of their dissertation by this point in the program."

She leaned left to gaze around me. "You might be the first person I've known who has actually read *Mein Kampf*."

"From your tone, I can tell that doesn't impress you at all. Just think, though, if people back then had read it — I mean *really* read it, all of it — the war and the camps might have been avoided. All Germany had to do was kick Hitler out."

"Kick him out?"

"He was Austrian, not German," I explained, after swallowing a mouthful of sesame chicken.

"Oh." Her eyes clouded over.

"Hindsight is twenty-twenty. What's your favorite book?" I realized I had droned on too much about Nazis. Historians weren't known for being suave.

"*Cannery Row*."

"Steinbeck. That's a great book. My favorite of his is *The Grapes of Wrath*."

"You read more than history texts?" Frivolity returned to her voice.

"Shocking, I know."

"Of course, Steinbeck's novels do have a certain level of historical and sociological appeal."

"Very true and an impressive assessment." Was she always so observant?

She flashed a victorious smile as if answering my unasked question.

I wasn't sure how to broach the subject, so I dove in headfirst. "You've determined that I haven't dated much since the *big breakup*." I made quote marks in the air in hopes to convey the ending of my relationship wasn't all that dramatic. "How about you?"

"Trying to figure out if I'm a sure thing tonight?" She tapped her nails against a wineglass.

"Wh — you're pulling my leg, aren't you?" I closed one eye, praying to the dating gods I was right.

"Maybe. Maybe not."

"The suspense is killing me." I set down my chopsticks.

"I bet it is." She stared me down for thirteen seconds. I knew because I counted. "To answer your question, my last relationship wasn't all that special, really. No major heartache on either side. It was fun for a few months, but it wasn't going anywhere."

"How long ago did it end?"

"Right before I met you."

"Does that make me your rebound?"

"Do you want to be my rebound?"

"Ha! I feel like I'm on a therapist's couch. Do you always respond with a question?"

"I don't know. Do I?" She grinned, obviously enjoying toying with me.

Strangely, I liked it.

Again we grew quiet, enjoying the meal.

"Are you cold?" I asked, noticing her shivering.

"A little." She nodded bashfully.

"I'm sorry. I'm usually very warm, so I keep the heat low." I motioned for her to pick up her plate. "Let's finish in front of the fireplace."

Balancing her plate and wineglass, she asked, "Won't that make you too hot?"

"I'll just take off my clothes." My cheeks burned at my unintentional *faux pas*. "I mean my sweater."

"I preferred your first response." She nudged me with her shoulder.

"There's a price for that."

Sarah hiked up an eyebrow. "Really? And what's that?"

"You have to stay the night."

"Pour some more wine and it's a deal."

She settled on the floor next to the fireplace. Orange firelight danced in her dark eyes. It took every ounce of control for me to not to lean over and kiss her right then and there.

Maybe it was her, but it didn't take long for the temperature to get to me. I set my plate down on my coffee table and yanked my sweater over my head. My T-shirt underneath hitched up, and I was sure I had just exposed more than my stomach, taut by all the hours spent on a bike.

"I wasn't expecting that," she murmured in a tone that didn't give any indication what she was referring to.

"I told you I get hot easily."

She smiled. "Not that. I wasn't expecting you to have a sexy bra on."

I shrugged, embarrassed. Soon after meeting Sarah I went lingerie shopping. I almost asked Ethan to go with me, but luckily there are countless articles on the Internet about what turns people on.

"Soft, sexy, purple ... did I spot some Chantilly lace?"

"Maybe."

Sarah put her plate aside and scooted over to sit right in front of me. "So you aren't completely clueless, then?"

She didn't wait for a response. Stroking my cheek with one fingertip, she traced down the side of my face and continued until she reached the top of my shirt. Playfully, she tugged the T-shirt up for a glimpse.

"This won't do," she muttered, and before I knew what was happening, she'd ripped it up over my head. "It *is* Chantilly lace."

"And you?"

"No lace."

"I have a feeling, though, that it's not your everyday bra." My breathing increased as I watched Sarah eyeing my chest as it moved up and down.

"I don't do everyday bras. Never ever."

She didn't instruct me to find out for myself, but her smirk screamed it. Gently, I pulled off her sweater and started to undo her button-up. She studied me as I patiently freed her body. I felt like I was at a museum, savoring the parts of a Grecian statue, revealing one inch at a time. Neither of us was in a rush. Spying a hint of red, I popped another button and revealed a crimson bra with black Japanese script on the cups. It sent my pussy into a tizzy, but I didn't want her to know that just yet.

The next button revealed her toned stomach. Finally, I popped the last one and eased the shirt right off. Goose bumps formed on her skin; I trailed a finger across her belly, and they multiplied.

"Cold?" I murmured.

She shook her head, her chocolate eyes imploring me to kiss her. I leaned closer, feeling her breath. This was the moment I had wanted since I met her: that moment before making love. Time to explore her body with my hands and tongue. It reminded me of Michelangelo's painting of Adam and God — Adam's lifeless finger reaching out to God's for the spark that would bring humankind into existence. That inch of space between Adam's finger and God's might be one of the most powerful blank spaces ever created.

There was an inch between my mouth and Sarah's. I smiled, knowing my grin exuded sheer happiness and so much promise.

"What are you waiting for?" she whispered.

I desired her spark. "You. I've been waiting for you."

Our mouths came together, soft and then hard. I deepened the kiss, and Sarah's gentle moan urged me on. She lay down on the floor, and I moved on top of her, her skin pressed against mine, electrifying all of my nerve endings.

I reached behind her and unclasped her bra. Her breasts were soft and full, her nipples resembling delicate pink buttons. Her left breast proudly bore one single freckle. My thumb circled the freckle and then her hardening nipple as we kissed again.

Moving to her other breast, I caressed her nipple with my tongue. Sarah's back arched, and she reached up and freed my hair from its ponytail holder. She ran her hands through my hair while my fingers trailed her stomach.

When she moved to undo her jeans, I stopped her. I wanted the pleasure of undressing her completely. Her panties matched her bra, as I'd suspected they would, and I teased a finger over the silk, feeling how warm she was, how wet, how almost ready for me.

I slipped the red panties slowly down her legs, noticing the wetness shimmering on her thighs. I wanted to taste her. Wanted to be inside her.

Not yet.

I raised her foot and sucked on her toes, then traced a hand up and down her firm calf. Her legs were smooth, supple, and stubble-free. She had prepared for this night, as had I.

The faintest smile played on her lips as if she had been reading my mind. Then she nodded. "Yes," she whispered.

My tongue slid its way up her leg, pausing right before her pussy. I could smell her – so sensual. I inhaled deeply. This was what it felt like to be completely alive, with all senses on high alert.

Moving to her other thigh, I licked my way to the place I could tell she wanted me. Her hips arched, calling me.

I opened her slick lips with careful fingers and eased a finger inside. Sarah let out a sexy, come-hither whimper.

Keeping my finger inside, I moved up to kiss her again, thrilled by the sensation of her tightening around my finger. We continued kissing, my finger moving in and out of her. Sensing she wanted more, I worked my way back down, detouring at one nipple and then the other.

Down and down my mouth explored.

I eased another finger inside her and flicked her clit with my tongue.

"Fuck, Lizzie. You feel so good." Her hands fisted my hair.

My fingers slid in and out slowly, my mouth and lips focused on her bundle of nerves. She was getting wetter by the second, and the movement of my hand was getting more frantic. Sarah's hips gyrated, forcing me to make an effort to keep my mouth where she wanted it. Truth be known, it would have taken a madman with a shotgun to get me to stop. Actually, even that wouldn't have stopped me from making love to Sarah.

I was falling for the way she moved. For her taste. For her soft moans.

Her breathing quickened; she was so close to coming. Her upper body jolted off the carpet and she let out a shriek that told me not to stop, even if the house caught on fire.

I plunged in as deep as I could go. Her nails dug into my back as she groaned and sighed.

Her body trembled, and I held my tongue and fingers in the same spot, relishing the vibrations of her orgasm as they progressed through her body. Sarah pushed my head deeper until I could barely breathe — not that I minded.

When the second aftershock stilled, she fell back onto the carpet. I plucked an afghan off the closest chair and spread it over us. She didn't move, so I held her; her hair smelled sweet, mussed on my shoulder.

"That was amazing," she said.

"Anything for you."

"I like the sound of that." She pulled my face to hers and kissed me. "I like tasting me on your tongue."

That got me going. I reached down to be inside her again, but she swatted my hand away. "No. My turn."

She flipped me on my back, hovering over me, her eyes feasting on my body. "Hard to believe you can eat so much and stay this fit." She stroked down from my neck to the waistline of my jeans. Without a word, she slipped my jeans off and removed my panties. "I wondered."

"If they matched?"

She nodded.

They did.

"Tell me. Is the cluelessness just an act?" She placed her hand over my crotch as if holding my pussy hostage.

"I wish it was."

Tilting her head back, she laughed heartily. She looked sexy as hell. I motioned for her to kiss me. "I can't get enough of you," I murmured.

The way she responded to my kiss suggested she felt the same.

I flinched as her fingers parted my lips below, and she entered me.

"And I have a feeling I won't ever get enough of you fucking me."

Sarah pushed in deeper, and I tossed my head back. "Please," I whispered.

"Anything for you." She nibbled on my earlobe, causing me to moan. My ears and neck were my favorite erogenous zones. She took note. I sensed she was an excellent student as well as a teacher.

Her tongue explored my body in a way no one else's had, each passing second heightening my emotions.

When she licked my clit, sucking it into her mouth, I nearly shouted in rapture. Sarah circled my bud, pushing me closer and closer to The Big O.

"Oh fuck, this feels incredible."

Her eyes flickered to mine; even with the firelight gleaming in them, they mirrored the intensity stirring in my body and mind.

Chapter Ten

"A girl stayed at my place last weekend," I casually told Ethan as he sat across from me in Starbucks.

"Is that what you call it?" was his glib reply.

I wrinkled my brow. "Call what?"

"Masturbation."

"Oh, hardy har har."

"What's your blowup doll's name?"

"You are on a roll today." I took a loud, angry slurp of my chai, just to annoy him.

"You keep setting them up, and I'll keep knocking them down." He tugged on the corner of his thin moustache.

"Please, I'm not easy."

"That's not what I heard." He mimicked smashing the cymbals of a drum kit and then said, "Ta dum da!'" His awkwardness made the action even funnier.

I sucked my bottom lip, trying not to laugh. "Just because you don't like sex doesn't mean the rest of us don't."

"Neanderthals. All of you!" He giggled foolishly.

"You sure do enjoy discussing my sex life."

"Because it gets you all riled up. I like watching you squirm."

"I don't squirm."

"Sarah might prefer it if you move more. Missionary lesbian sex, I imagine, doesn't impress the ladies."

"What?"

"You'll need to do more than just dry hump her leg."

I choked on my chai.

He mimicked a theatrical bow while staying seated, took a moment to catch his breath, and then said, "How cute that you said a girl stayed at your place."

"Why is that cute?"

"You're trying so hard to keep your emotions in check. Trying to separate your heart from Lizzie logic, but you're falling for her, aren't you? And I'm referring to Sarah, of course, not some random girl you had over." He winked.

"Lizzie logic?"

He didn't respond. Instead, he stared me down. He'd mastered this tactic back at school and it still worked.

"Whatever," I said.

"Ha! I knew I was right. Not that you would admit it. Feeling a little scared, Miss Lizzie?" Ethan let his Southern accent slip in, and then he chuckled maliciously.

"You're full of yourself today," I said, aware that he was making me uncomfortable. "What's going on?"

"I paid off my student loan last week. I feel free." He reached for the sky with both hands.

Ethan and I had started grad school together. Initially, he had been pursuing a PhD in Twentieth Century Literature, but he'd quit two years after earning his master's. I'd hoped he might go back and finish his doctorate one day. It seemed the chance of that happening just got slimmer. But I knew that debt weighed heavily on him. It was no secret he and his wife didn't make a lot of money.

"What? How?"

"My grandfather died — "

"I'm so sorry!" I hadn't even known his grandfather was ill.

"Don't be. He was an asshole. But a rich asshole." He tapped his fingers together Scrooge-like.

"That's great, then. I'm happy for you." I tried to pretend I wasn't still disappointed that he'd quit. During his master's, we'd been inseparable, helping each other through many all-nighters. We were in different departments, of course, but we both focused on the same time period and loved to bounce ideas off each other. When he'd given up, I'd felt abandoned and we even stopped speaking for a while. When we'd run into each other months later and gone for coffee, I'd discovered I still enjoyed being around him.

After my relationship with Meg crashed and burned, Ethan had been there for me. His marriage hadn't been stable at the time either. Before, we'd bonded over graduate-school stress. Now, coping with everyday life was the issue that brought us together once a week.

"Oh, are you still mad?" He waggled his eyebrows.

"What? No. Of course not. You want another?" I stood to order a second chai.

"Sure. My usual, please."

"One plain cup of Joe coming up."

When I returned, he set his book aside. Despite having quit his program, Ethan always had his nose buried in a book; I admired that about him.

"So, I have confirmation." I stared into Ethan's eyes, after retaking my seat. "I'm not a bad lay."

Coffee spewed out of one corner of his mouth, and he wiped it off the table with a napkin. "And who, exactly, confirmed this for you?"

"Sarah, of course." I took a careful sip of my chai, which was still scorching hot.

"How do you know *Sarah* isn't lying?" The trace of a sneer made the corners of his lips curl.

"Don't start with the whole Sally thing again."

He slapped the table. "I *knew* you'd watch the film. You are such a nerd! You'll *research* anything." Even though he didn't make air quotes, I felt them in his tone.

"I should thank you, actually. I watched the film with Sarah. And then we watched *Casablanca*. Of course, now she thinks I love romantic movies and she wants to do another marathon this weekend."

"Two movies don't equate to a marathon. Do you have to pick out the rom-coms?"

"What's a rom-com?" I frowned at him.

Ethan groaned. "Okay, let me help you. Rom-com is short for romantic comedy — films that are lighthearted, funny, and focus on true love no matter the obstacle. Think *Love Actually*."

My face betrayed me.

"You haven't seen *Love Actually*?" He was speechless. "Good Lord! How is it that I know more about chick flicks than you do?"

"Your wife, maybe."

"Lisa's not a fan of them, actually." His frown showed his disappointment.

"But you are?"

"I won't lie. I enjoy a good rom-com from time to time." Ethan seized my journal and clicked the pen. "Here's a list to get you through." He scratched the cap of the pen against his cheek after each entry, putting much thought into the selection. A few moments later, he handed me the list. No wonder people thought he was gay.

I scanned it. "I don't know any of these." I mouthed the titles as I read: *Moonstruck, You've Got Mail, Notting Hill, Bridget Jones's*

Diary, Four Weddings and a Funeral.

"Why did you list the last one? That doesn't sound romantic or funny."

"You have to trust me on this." He thumped the list.

"What about *Bringing up Baby* and *The Philadelphia Story*? I like those. Surely screwball comedies count."

"Only as backup. Not as the only movies." He narrowed his eyes. "Do you understand? Not everyone loves classics like you do."

"Okay, geez. Whatcha reading?" I gestured to his book.

"*Thank You, Jeeves.*"

"Funny. Sarah asked me where I hid Jeeves when she was at my place."

He sighed. "You mentioned Miranda, didn't you? Seriously. You need to stop telling people you have a cleaning lady." He punctuated each word with a nod of his head. "It's weird for someone your age."

"What's wrong with wanting a clean place?"

"Nothing. If I could afford it – "

I started to speak, but Ethan's glare forced me to suck my words back.

"Don't pimp out Miranda."

As per usual, he was dead-on. I had been about to offer to pay for her to clean Ethan's place once a week. He hated it when I did things like that. I'd never understood his sensitivities about money. Of course, I'd always had money. I had never known what it was like to live paycheck to paycheck. Last year, I'd helped him pay for a new transmission for Lisa's car. The conversation hadn't been pretty, but in the end, Ethan had let me help. He had to really.

"You act like an old lady sometimes. I'm surprised you don't wear lace shirts with frilly collars. Not that *that* is much better."

He gestured to my outfit, and I had a feeling he was trying to steer the conversation to safer waters.

I peered down at my sweater-vest and jeans — my typical uniform on days I wasn't lecturing. "You're an old lady," I said, knowing full well how meek I sounded.

"Does Sarah dress like you?"

"No way. She's hot!" A grin spread across my face.

"You see!"

"But I can't dress like her. I'd feel foolish. She has the body for it." I outlined a curvy body to emphasize my point.

He laughed. "Maybe just ditch the sweater-vest for a while. Try wearing a normal sweater."

"I did the night Sarah was over."

"And you got laid. See how that works." He winked.

"She told me she likes that I'm clueless."

Ethan burst into a fit of chuckles. "Oh boy, that's funny. And lucky. Careful, Lizzie, you might actually keep this one."

"What do you mean?"

"I know you. All those years you dated Meg, even though she spent most of her time at your place, she never moved in with you. I bet she never even had a key." He boosted one eyebrow over the rim of his glasses.

I blinked and then swallowed hard.

"What did you say before, 'People like me don't fall in love?' I have a feeling commitment isn't your thang." His Southern twang twisted the final word.

"I don't remember saying that." However, I had to admit it sounded exactly like something I would say. I took pride in not needing others in my life. And I feared how Sarah would react if she found out about my obscene amount of money. Meg was still in my life because I was rich.

"Not too long after we met, when I told you I was married,

you said it for the first time. You should have seen the disgust on your face." He waved liked he was shooing away a gnat. "I already knew you well enough not to be insulted."

"Do you think that's true? I'm a commitment-phobe?" Realizing I was blinking excessively, I tried to steady my eyelids. When my eyes started to water, I realized I wasn't blinking at all.

Ethan watched, bemused. "It doesn't matter what I think. It matters what you think, and how you react to a serious relationship. One word comes to mind: sabotage."

"Sounds like a Hitchcock movie." I rubbed my temple. "I think he made one called *Sabotage* and another called *Saboteur*."

Ethan gulped some air, rolled his eyes, and swiped a stray hair off his shoulder. "Sarah's right. You really are clueless."

"Have any of your students ever tried to kill themselves?"

"What?" He plunked his cup down.

"One of Sarah's students tried to kill herself last week," I explained.

"Oh. How awful." He shook his head. "Nope. Not to my knowledge. Is she close to the kid?"

I nodded. "I think she's close with a lot of her students. That's how we met."

"A high school student introduced you? You're kidding!" He chuckled.

"No, you idiot. She organizes visits to college campuses to encourage at-risk students to apply. She also coaches volleyball."

"Ah, she's one of those."

"What do you mean?"

"An overachiever. You two are perfect for each other."

"What? Don't you volunteer?"

"Volunteer? Teachers get paid for those things. Not a lot, though. Not enough for me to figure out how to coach some lame sport like badminton."

I tried picturing Ethan coaching any sport; I couldn't. Is that why Sarah was always so busy with school activities? Trying to earn extra dough?

"What about debate? You love to argue with me."

"Please. You're easy pickings!"

This made me laugh. "Do you think she's poor just because she's a teacher? She shops a lot."

He scratched the side of his nose. "Please don't ask her that. Not everyone is so flippant about money matters."

I sighed. Ethan was right. I couldn't ask her why she shopped so much when she couldn't afford a car. It was none of my business. A thought struck me. Maybe her mother paid for everything. Did moms do that? Mine was probably still pissed she had to feed and clothe me until I was of age, but maybe that wasn't the case for all daughters. Was that why Sarah spent every Saturday with her mother? Free shit? Okay, that thought didn't make it any better.

Chapter Eleven

"LIZZIE, TRY THIS ON," I sat up, naked, and slipped on a lilac sweater-vest Sarah had retrieved from one of the spilled shopping bags. After her usual shopping spree with her mother, she had popped by my apartment. Before I knew it, we were in bed together.

"Oh, this is soft." I hugged the vest, loving the sensation against my bare skin.

Sarah held my arms to the side and inspected her purchase. "Not bad. Shows off your curves a bit more."

"Curves? Please." I crossed my arms.

She yanked them apart and cupped one of my boobs. "Yes, this is a curve. A very nice curve, I might add." Her other hand slipped under me to grab my ass. "This is another."

I responded by pulling her on top of me.

"I might have to buy you more gifts if you always respond this way."

"No need to buy me gifts. I know you're saving for a new car. I can think of other ways to get me revved up."

Sarah quirked a sexy eyebrow.

She was still wet from earlier, allowing my fingers easy access. Her eyes closed and she sighed as I nuzzled her breast with my nose.

"Now this is a curve," I said. Her nipple rose to attention. "And I love this." I took it in my mouth. Down below, I thrust my fingers in and out of her. "Oh, and the way your hips move when I'm inside you ... it's ... absolutely incredible."

Sarah slid her hands around my neck and pulled my face down to hers. Her ragged breath inspired my fingers to probe deeper. Biting her lower lip, she watched me intently.

"Come for me. I love your face when you come."

"I love — " She couldn't get the rest of the words out.

"NOW, THAT SWEATER-VEST looks good on you. Did you go shopping?" Ethan stirred more sugar into his coffee.

"Uh, no. Sarah bought it for me."

"Sarah bought you a sweater-vest? So you do wear them around her. I thought we talked about this." He waggled a wooden stir stick jokingly in my face.

I put my palms up in mock surrender. "I was wearing one when she met me, and the other night she surprised me at my place, so of course I had one on then." Actually, I'd worn them around her more often than I cared to admit.

"Of course." He smiled wryly. "How many do you own?"

"One more this week," I answered.

"*Touché*," he retorted and leaned over to rub the fabric. "Soft. Cashmere soft."

"What? No. It can't be."

He motioned for me to lean over. When I did, he flipped the tag out for a better view. "Yep. Cashmere."

"What? That doesn't make sense. She doesn't have the money for this. Why is she buying me this?"

"How do you know she doesn't have money?"

"She teaches high school English," I said.

Ethan scowled; then a faint smile made an appearance. "I

see. From my experience as a high school English teacher that's true."

"I'm sorry, Ethan. I speak — "

"Without thinking. I'm aware. Who does she shop with? I know it's not you."

"Her mom."

"Maybe her mom pays for everything. Mine still splurges on me once in a while."

"You think this is a gift from her mom?" The idea was unsettling.

"Not necessarily. I'm just saying you don't know how much of her own money she actually spends."

Several awkward seconds slipped by. "Should I give it back, just in case?"

Ethan was lost in thought. "What?"

I tugged at my vest.

"No. You should not give back a gift and say, 'You're a poor teacher. You can't afford this.'"

"I have to pay her back. Or maybe — "

He put his palm to his forehead to cut me off. "Or what? Trust me, whatever thought just popped into your head, forget it."

I grunted.

Ethan's eyes widened.

"I wasn't thinking anything." I spoke to my lap.

He brushed my hand, and I met his gaze, softened behind his thick lenses. "Listen, I know money holds no value for you, since you have more than God, but it's a sensitive subject for those of us who have to sell our souls to make a penny or two."

I remained mute.

"Do not offer her cash or a check. You have to trust her."

I shifted in my chair. He had no idea about Meg's demands

for money. I pushed the thought out of my head. "But this doesn't make sense. Her car broke down, and she needs a new one. Why is she buying me this when she needs a new car? I have to pay her back. Her mom drives her back and forth to work. Maybe – "

He silenced me with a crisp shake of the head. "No. Do not think of buying her a car. Out of the question." Ethan chomped down on his lower lip.

"I wasn't thinking that."

He cocked his head, daring me to explain.

"I was going to rent a car for her," I said, still to my lap.

"Do not offer to buy her a car. Do not offer to rent her a car. She's a grown woman. You have to trust her."

"Am I allowed to drive her to work and pick her up? Sometimes she stays the night at my place," I mumbled.

"Do you ever stay at her place?"

"Rarely."

"Why don't you stay at her place more?"

"In Loveland?"

He shook his head. "Yes. You know that's where I live, right?"

"I didn't mean it like that. Her apartment isn't very nice, and it's old. I'm getting the heebie-jeebies thinking about it. Who knows how many people lived there before?"

My apartment was brand-new when I moved in.

"Are you afraid of ghosts?"

"No. Germs."

"Such a priss."

"Says the man who only shits in his own home."

He flashed his you-got-me grin.

"She says she prefers my place since its newer and sparkling clean." I did too, not that I would tell Sarah that, but I think she knew my true feelings. She had walked into the bathroom unannounced while I was squatting a good three inches over her toilet seat.

Ethan's forehead scrunched. "Okay, so how often is she staying over?"

"A couple nights a week." I squirmed in my seat. Ever since the first weekend she'd stayed, it was more than two nights.

"Oh, good Lord! Is this a U-Haul lesbian thing?" He chuckled.

"A U-what?" I cocked my head.

"A U-Haul Lesbian." He studied my face and then howled with laughter. "You don't know that term?" He lifted his frames and dabbed his eyes with the cuff of his sweater. "I swear I'm gayer than you."

"What are you talking about? Is U-Haul a gay-owned company?"

That made him bellow with laughter even more. When his mirth subsided, he explained. "Lesbians are known for moving in together after a couple of dates. That's why they're called U-Haul lesbians, because after their second date they move in together." He watched closely to make sure I was connecting the dots. "Understand?"

"That's absurd! Why would two rational adults rush into things?"

"That may be the case, but if you plan on getting back into the lesbian world, you might want to brush up on the lingo."

"Lesbian world? What do you mean?" I rubbed my chin.

"When's the last time you went on a date? Not including Sarah."

"Not since Meg. You already know that."

"You two broke up over a year ago." Despite the topic, he had a compassionate air. "I know she ripped your heart out, and it's good to see you're getting past it. Not all women are evil."

"Ripped my heart out," I repeated with derision, swatting his words away like puffs of air. Even Ethan didn't know all the details about Meg. "Whatever. And I know all about evil women."

"I'm not talking about your mom. You can't run from relationships."

"*Run from relationships*," I parroted. "I don't. I never miss one of our meetings." I rapped on the tabletop.

"Meetings." He rolled his eyes. "You're so charming sometimes. I'm not talking about friendships, even if I'm your only friend. You can't just live with your work. Get out of your office, including the one in your home. Live a little!" His dreamy look made me wonder if he was talking to me or himself.

Chapter Twelve

MY EYES POPPED OPEN RIGHT before five in the morning. Sarah snored softly next to me, her head on my shoulder. It was Sunday, and I was dying to get on my bike. I usually rode at least twenty miles every morning, unless Sarah stayed the night. Since she'd started sleeping over most nights a little over a month ago, I'd been feeling restless.

I edged her head onto the pillow, holding my breath. She stirred but settled down right away. Without turning the lights on, I tiptoed out of my bedroom and changed in the bathroom. Part of me felt silly, slipping out of my own apartment. The other part screamed for me to get on my bike and ride.

It was freezing out. Frigid spring wind slashed through my clothes, and my lungs burned when I breathed, expelling a trail of vapor. But it was energizing, and my body and mind craved it. Ever since I could remember, I needed daily doses of strenuous exercise. Hiking used to be my go-to, until I was struck with Graves' disease. It caused leg weakness, making hiking difficult and dangerous since I preferred going alone. I started riding regularly soon after my diagnosis years ago. Riding pushed me to my limits, but not past them. Unless it was snowing out, I was on my bike every morning – until recently, at least. Occasionally, I would hike on the weekends, but never the strenuous hikes I used to enjoy.

Two hours later, I cautiously reentered my apartment, stopping to assess the situation. All was quiet. I slipped into the bedroom, relieved to see Sarah in the same position she had been in when I left. How was that possible? I was an insomniac. Any slight movement or sound woke me, and even when I was asleep I tossed and turned.

Not wanting to crawl back into bed sweaty, I stepped into the shower. The hot water burned my frozen fingers and toes. Normally, I let my body temperature regulate before getting in, avoiding the tingling pain of boiling water on frozen body parts. After a quick rinse, I shut the water off, wiggled my digits to counteract the tingling sensation, and then toweled off and slipped into my pajamas. Hopefully, Sarah would have forgotten I'd fallen asleep naked next to her, like I did even on the nights we didn't make love.

I pulled back the covers and slid into bed as best I could, trying not to jostle her.

"Why is your hair wet?" she said, in a voice thick with sleep.

"I took a shower," I explained, hoping she was groggy enough to doze off again.

"Why?"

"I, uh ... went out for a bit, and when I got back, I took a shower to warm up."

"It's Sunday. Where'd you go?" She sat up in bed.

Was I in trouble? "I went for a bike ride."

"This early?" she asked in an incredulous tone.

"I usually go every morning."

She frowned. "This is the first time since I've been here that you have."

"Well, I thought it would be rude."

"Rude? How?"

"It's bad manners to ditch a guest in your home."

"Guest." She chortled. "You're funny." Sarah eyeballed me. "Go on your bike rides. I love the results." She winked and attempted to pinch my ass. Too quick for her, I pinned her to the bed.

"Really?" I said.

"Yes. Very much."

I leaned down to kiss her, but she dodged my lips. "Morning breath."

"I brushed and rinsed." I breathed into my hand to reassure myself.

"Not you. Me."

"Ask me if I care."

"I do." She covered her mouth with the back of her hand.

I nodded. "Okay. Can I do this?" I kissed her forehead and then the tip of her nose. Skipping her mouth, I worked my way down her neck and found her nipple waiting for me. It sprang to life in my mouth. I bit it gently and then harder. Sarah writhed under me, urging me further down her body. Peppering her stomach with kisses, I licked her clit briefly before continuing my trek down her body. Her moans suggested she was angry and excited all at once. I loved taking my time with Sarah. There wasn't an inch of her body I hadn't explored, but each time felt fresh. It was hard to imagine not wanting to make love to her over and over again.

She also loved to tease me. While I trailed kisses down the inside of one thigh, I watched her massage her clit with a finger, curious to see how far she'd take it. She noticed my interest. I'm not sure which of us felt more aroused as she slid a finger inside herself.

I sucked in air, gasping as Sarah fingered herself deeper,

seductively plunging in and out. Her other hand concentrated on circling her clit. I could not tear my eyes away from her smooth, sexy motions.

"Join me," she whispered, her voice breathy.

I moved to lap at her clit, but Sarah shook her head. "Please touch yourself."

I froze. I'd never done that in front of anyone before.

She smiled. "Come on. Do it for me?" All the while, she never stopped fucking herself. I was bursting for release.

Two could play at this game. Hovering over her face, I started to rub myself. Sarah's eyes widened. Encouraged by her response, I shoved one finger inside, the rest focusing on my pulsing bud. Sarah's fingers moved even more frantically below, and I reciprocated.

"Come for me. Oh God, come!" she exclaimed. Her hips rose all the way off the bed, and I pleasured myself with fury, throwing my head back, equally close to coming. Beneath me, Sarah's body trembled and bucked.

"I need to taste you," she growled before tossing me onto my back and planting her head between my legs.

The first lick of her warm tongue sent a sensation jolting through me that I swear I'd never felt before. It was as if she was the first person to ever make love to me.

"Oh," I moaned, my head lolled over the side of the bed, my eyes closing. "Please don't stop, whatever you do."

Sarah's hands gripped my thighs as her tongue continued to explore.

The orgasm hit me hard. My entire body shook and arched as if I'd just stuck a finger in a light socket. Sarah still never stopped licking me. A second wave hit and then a third. Finally, she held her tongue absolutely still as I came again.

"Jesus fucking Christ!" The words slipped out of my mouth.

She entwined her arms with mine. "I love it when you come."

Exhausted, I managed to gasp out, "Why?"

"Because you let me in completely."

I had a feeling she didn't mean her fingers and tongue. I knew she'd just felt a connection to my soul, because I had too, although I didn't say it.

I shivered.

"Aftershock?" She giggled.

I said nothing. Let her think that.

LATER THAT DAY, we popped into the Starbucks next to the theater. Our movie wouldn't start for another forty minutes, and the lobby was crammed with screaming kids, so we'd opted to wait outside, staying warm with our hot drinks.

"What other secrets do you keep?" Sarah asked out of the blue. She fished in her coat pocket for the sugar packets she'd stuffed in there.

"I'm sorry?"

"Besides bike riding." She stirred raw sugar into her coffee.

"Going for bike rides counts as having secrets?" I tapped the side of my chai.

"Not telling me that you ride, yes." She tickled my thigh, letting me know she wasn't overly concerned.

"I'm an open book," I said with as much conviction as possible.

"Ha! Let me see your eyes."

I leveled my gaze on her lovely face.

"Nope, you don't even believe that hogwash."

I had to laugh. "What can I say? I don't open up quickly."

"Let's start with the basics. Tell me about your family."

"Ah, you see, there's not much to tell. We're not close."

She shook her head, exasperated. "I know. But why?"

Why? What good could come from opening that Pandora's box?

I sighed. "They don't like me much, and vice versa." I shifted on the ledge where we sat.

"Is it because you're gay?"

"Partly," I replied, evasive. "Let's talk about something cheerful."

"Such as?" She waited expectantly.

"Puppies and kittens," I offered, knowing full well I had just failed one of her tests.

Luckily for me, a gaggle of girls rushed out of the lobby, each one wearing a red wig, distracting us.

"What's that about?" I asked.

"They probably just saw *Brave*." Sarah waited a moment, before adding, "The movie."

"Ah," I said as if I knew what she was talking about.

Her phone beeped. Out of the corner of my eye I tried determining her mood as she quickly scanned the text. I couldn't. There went my career as a spy. Sarah slipped the phone into her back pocket.

Part of me wanted to point out that she was slightly hypocritical. She'd just questioned me about the so-called secret bike rides, but she never told me who was calling or texting her twenty-four seven. Of course, I didn't expect her to. Meg used to interrogate the shit out of me about any human contact.

She nudged my arm. "I think we can find a spot inside now," she said, her words sending a puff of vapor into the air.

"Great. Let's get some popcorn." I stood and swung the door open for her.

"What if we eat it all before the movie starts?" I waved the silly thought aside. "I'll get more, of course."

"It still amazes me how much you can eat," Sarah made of show of checking out my ass, "and stay so skinny."

I smiled. "Quick, grab that bench over there. I'll get the snacks."

"Don't forget the Milk Duds," she shouted after me, and I acknowledged it with a wave.

After getting the loot, I took a seat next to her on the bench. I tended to arrive ridiculously early for things, and now Sarah was being patient even though earlier she'd teased that I wanted to hurry up to wait. "I thought of something while in line. It doesn't count as a secret, but ..." I shrugged. "I once told a woman about my illness and she said I was lucky to be able to eat so much. It was back when my Graves was in high gear. I was eating seven to eight full meals a day, and I always felt like I was starving to death. I wanted to pop her in the nose. I know my illness isn't well-known, and I won't die from it, but it still changed my life ... drastically. For her to say I was lucky ..." I shook my head and took a sip of my chai.

Sarah placed a sympathetic hand on my arm, gave it a squeeze, and then shoved popcorn into her mouth, flashing a guilty smile. "Were you awfully sick?" she asked in a sweet, concerned tone. Her fingers stroked my knuckles.

I nodded. "It wasn't fun. I asked countless doctors for help. When one doctor reported that the latest round of tests showed nothing, I broke down in tears in his office. He asked me if I'd *wanted* something to be wrong with me. As if I wanted to be sick." I snorted, remembering the frustration. "I didn't know how to explain to him that I *knew* there was something wrong with me, but he and the rest of them just didn't care enough to find out what it was."

"Is there a cure?" Sarah set her coffee down on the bench, intent on my answer. She didn't seem to notice or care that we were sitting in the lobby of a crowded theater discussing my thyroid disease. I wasn't one to open up much, and now that I'd opened the door, Sarah showed no intention of dropping the subject.

I shook my head. "Treatment with the chance of remission."

"Are you close to remission?"

"My numbers are improving. I have a blood test in a couple of weeks. Cross your fingers."

"I will." Sarah's eyes grew misty, which made me feel miserable. She'd wanted me to share, and I had, but I'd told her something that made her cry.

"Who was taking care of you when you were ... sick?"

I laughed. "Me. It all came to a head after the big breakup." Meg never accepted that I was ill. Instead, she'd accused me of faking it to make her feel guilty. I responded by hiding my symptoms and ignoring signs, such as a rapid heartbeat and dramatic weight loss. I dropped twenty pounds in a little over a month. "More than likely, the problem surfaced during undergrad, but it didn't become full-blown until years later."

"Do you think the stress from the breakup pushed it along?"

I hitched a shoulder. "It probably didn't help; that's for sure. And being a grad student adds to my stress levels." I didn't like that we were veering into uncomfortable Meg memories.

"You really do need someone to care of you." Her face told me I'd found that someone.

Then I saw something that made my head spin.

Meg. Surely I was imagining her.

I blinked.

It couldn't be. Was the money-grubbing psycho stalking me?

She stood on the other side of the lobby, watching me intently. *This can't be happening.* The last thing I needed was for Sarah to meet Meg-the-Destroyer again. I wasn't a dating expert, but having the ex and current girlfriend in the same building spelled disaster — even for someone as inexperienced as me.

"Would you excuse me for a moment?" I sprung up like a jack-in-the-box on speed.

Sarah nodded. I placed a hand on her shoulder as I passed and then focused on Meg.

She was inching closer. I dashed right by her, headed for the restroom. Under my breath I muttered, "Come."

When I reached the door to the bathroom, I rounded to see Meg standing in the same spot. She looked to Sarah and then back to me, repeating the action a couple more times before she followed.

Fortunately, Sarah was too engrossed in reading movie blurbs on the brochure we'd received when purchasing our tickets.

I pushed open the door and motioned for Meg to go ahead.

"Aren't you full of manners today," she said.

Miraculously, the bathroom was nearly deserted. One occupant was in the far stall, about fifteen doors down.

"Hi, Meg." I stared at the open stall behind me, imagining dunking her head in the toilet. How many times had I held her hair back? A hundred too many.

"Aren't you happy to see me?" she said through gritted teeth.

Totally below the belt. When I'd met Meg, she was a couple years ahead and I was fresh off receiving my master's. She was beautiful, intelligent, witty — everything I always wanted in a woman. I'd idolized her. At first, I even thought I could "save" her. But Meg didn't want to be saved. She wanted to obliterate everything in her path: her career, her family, me. In hindsight, I should have walked away after that first year.

But I hadn't. I'd thought she was the one.

She was a nightmare.

An absolute nightmare.

Not only was Meg an alcoholic, but she was also a mean one. The drunken invective that flew out of her mouth had scarred me for life and reminded me too much of my mother.

Even Ethan hadn't known the whole story. He knew she'd broken my heart, but he had no idea she'd also broken me. It was too hard to admit I'd been conned by her in the beginning — duped by her fake sweetness, intellect, and beauty. She'd made me feel special when no one else in my life ever had. It took me a full year after the relationship to realize she'd seen me as weak. I was easy prey for the likes of Meg.

All of this was way before she started demanding money from me. That didn't happen until after we split. At first, guilt urged me to give in to her demands. Was there such a thing as survivor's guilt when it came to leaving an alcoholic? The demands for money kept coming, and the amounts continued to increase. When I started hedging, Meg set me straight, so to speak. Actually she scared the crap out of me. All it took was one rumor about plagiarism or an inappropriate relationship with a student, and all of my hard work would be flushed down the toilet. Neither ever happened. That didn't stop Meg from threatening. The woman had no conscience. Now that she'd seen me twice with Sarah, I knew she had fresh ammunition against me.

Most people who knew me thought I was brilliant — clueless, sure, but still book smart and rational — but the whole Meg debacle proved I was just a weakling, desperate for love and acceptance.

After I left her (I told everyone she'd left me, hoping they would pity me enough to not ask too many questions) I'd been determined never to fall in love again. To avoid questions about what happened, I pretended to pine for Meg. I'd even told Ethan, on several occasions, that I would be with her again if given the chance. I can't remember how many times I pretended to be lovesick, when in reality I never wanted to see Meg again.

That didn't mean I forgot about her. I couldn't. Sometimes, when I saw a woman who reminded me of Meg, sadness would roost in my chest. There were times I missed the old Meg, the loving Meg — the one who made me feel special. The con artist Meg. She needed a chump like me to control, and I was desperate for someone to think I was worthy of love. It was a perfect storm, really.

For some time, I didn't think I would ever go on a date again. Then, when I saw Sarah in Dr. Marcel's office …

"Are you on a date?" Meg's question snapped me back to reality.

I didn't respond right away. Finally, I said, "What do you want? Money?"

"What's her name?"

"Doesn't matter."

"Does she know she doesn't matter?"

I remained mute.

A woman rushed past and slammed a stall door shut. Moments later, I heard her pissing. Seriously, could my life get any worse?

Meg tugged at a string on her sweater. "I'm thinking of coming back to school."

"That's wonderful." I forced a fake smile; all the while, the room was spinning. "I'm glad to see things are turning around for you."

She let out an angry snort. "Yeah, things are looking up. How about you? How's your dissertation?"

"Good, thanks." I'd long ago learned it was best to answer Meg's questions with the fewest words; it gave her less opportunity to twist things.

"Does she know about you? What you did to me?"

Meg always insisted I broke her. Before me, she was fine. She could handle everything. Somehow, I'd converted her into the monster she became.

"It was nice seeing you. I'm leaving." I wheeled around.

"Wait!" The desperation in her voice snared me back into her web.

I stopped, waiting for her to explain.

"I do."

Confusion clouded my vision.

"I do need money." At least she had the decency to avoid my gaze.

"Ah. Right. Text me." With that, I stormed out of the restroom. I should have known the real reason she cornered me in the john. If only I could detect a pattern to Meg's demands. Sometimes she'd ask a couple of times a month, and other times I wouldn't hear from her for weeks. Did she really need money this time, or was our run-in just too good of an opportunity to pass up? It didn't matter really as long as she left Sarah out of our situation.

Sarah remained on the bench. "You okay?" she asked when I sat down.

"Yeah ... no. I think I'll get a Sprite."

She tossed my chai in the trash can. "Let me get it. Why don't you wait outside and get some fresh air?"

"That's okay." I peered at the exit where Meg stood. "I'd rather be near you." I flashed a weak smile.

Sarah hooked her arm through mine and walked us to the shortest line. "You want to leave?"

It took much restraint not to glance over my shoulder to see if the coast was clear. "Nah, I'll be fine in a minute or two. Besides, I'm super excited to watch a movie about a talking teddy bear."

She whacked my arm. "Hey! That's not fair. When I suggested *Ted*, you said sure."

I leaned my head against hers, comforted by the fragrance of her shampoo. "Next time, I demand full disclosure. You knew I had no idea what it was about."

Oddly, her sweet, evil giggle put me at ease.

God, I hoped she was nothing like Meg.

If she was, it would crush me.

But Sarah never acted like Meg. Since we started spending almost every night together, I looked forward to seeing her each and every day. When Sarah had a glass of wine with dinner, she stopped before getting tipsy. And if she did get drunk, I never worried about my safety. Not once had she raised her voice. No threats. Never a shove. No arm on my throat while reading me the drunk riot act.

If she was running late, she'd let me know. If I was late, she'd say "poor baby" and offer to give me a shoulder rub, not interrogate me about who I was with or accuse me of seeing someone on the sly. Sarah trusted me. I was learning to trust her. Mostly. The fear of Sarah finding out about my trust fund lurked in the recesses of my mind.

Chapter Thirteen

MEG TEXTED ME SEVERAL DAYS later, asking for money. I knew I shouldn't have agreed, but I couldn't say no. For once, Ethan had other plans at our usual time, so I didn't tell Sarah and, instead, arranged to meet Meg at Frankie's in a small town north of Fort Collins, in the hope no one would see us. I didn't need any more rumors swirling about Meg. The past few years, with everyone thinking they knew everything, had been torture enough.

"Next time, maybe we could meet in Cheyenne," Meg said as she took her seat across from me.

How many more next times would there be?

"Sorry." I didn't know what else to say. She was the one who always insisted on cash. I didn't have PayPal or anything, but I'd set up an account in an instant if it meant not seeing Meg ever again.

Meg's beguiling green eyes bored into me. Her fake scarlet hair was swept into a ponytail. Her smile was false. I tried to remember whether her smile was always false.

"How are you?"

"You mean am I drinking?" She fiddled with a fork. "From what I saw that one night, you can't criticize. Never again."

I sighed.

"Your girlfriend is pretty."

"Thanks."

She cleared her throat. "So, you two are dating?"

I nodded. It was no use denying it. I feared if I did and Meg discovered otherwise, she'd make me pay through the nose.

"That's good. I'm happy for you." Her eyes told me the truth.

"What about you? Dating anyone?"

Meg snorted. "Nope." She looked away. "Just having fun and making ends meet."

Her demeanor set off alarm bells. "Having fun and making ends meet" — I didn't even want to fathom what that meant. Who else was she blackmailing?

I stifled a sigh. How was it that years ago I'd been with this woman and now we couldn't get through the basic pleasantries that arise when seeing someone after a long absence?

"I have your ..." I placed the envelope on the table.

She didn't move to take it.

"You're different."

I covered my mouth. Through the cracks of my fingers, I asked, "How so?"

"You seem happy. At peace."

I wish I could have said the same about her, but it was clear that angst controlled her.

I smiled awkwardly. "Thanks."

Meg didn't reply or move a muscle. It was unnerving.

"Have you spoken to Dr. Marcel yet?"

She tapped her manicured nails on the table. That was new. I'd never seen her wear nail polish ... and it was the black nail polish Janice mentioned. I almost laughed out loud thinking of Janice's outlandish thought that Meg was turning tricks. "Not ... yet."

I couldn't imagine what that conversation with Dr. Marcel

would entail. "I think it's great you want to move forward."

Meg stared into my eyes and then looked down at my hand. "Move forward? Is that what you call it?"

I flinched as though I'd been zapped.

"What do you call it?"

"I don't know what else to do with my life." She half shrugged.

"You're brilliant. No one can take that away from you." I had no idea why I was giving her a pep talk.

She tsked.

We stared at each other.

"Well, this was illuminating, as always." Meg snatched the envelope. "Have a great life, Lizzie."

After she left, I sat stunned in my seat, pondering whether I would ever see her again. Her last sentence held a touch of finality, but a sense of doom hung in the air. Nope, I was certain that wasn't the last of Meg, unfortunately. The money would run out, like always. Five hundred here and three hundred there didn't last long in today's world.

"Can I get you anything?" the waitress asked with kindness in her eyes. Maybe she'd sensed the emotional toll on me.

"Another chai, please."

"Coming right up. How about a cinnamon roll fresh from the oven?"

That made me smile. "Yes, please. And can I have two to go?"

SOON AFTER I returned home, Sarah bounded through the door.

"You're a sight for sore eyes."

"I missed you." I nuzzled into her arms. "I got you a treat."

Sarah disentangled herself. "What?"

"Cinnamon rolls from Frankie's."

"Yum. I'm famished."

"I'll make tea for us while you get settled." I waved to all her bags.

Minutes later, I heard, "Lizzie, come here, please."

I couldn't decide whether I was content or not that Sarah felt so at home in my apartment.

The front room was in complete shambles — bags and other items were strewn everywhere. Why did she love shopping so much? Shopping was an activity I avoided at all costs. I'd rather get a Brazilian wax; I wasn't entirely sure what that involved, but I had an inkling it was something I'd regret signing up for. Still, it was heads above shopping in my book. And I could afford it.

"What's up?"

She took my hand. "Come sit on the couch." I did. "Close your eyes."

"Why?" I didn't obey the last command.

"I want to try something. Close your eyes."

I regarded her warily.

Sarah laughed. "I'm not going to hurt you. Sheesh! Trust me, and close your eyes."

I wasn't happy she'd used the trust card. "Fine." I closed them.

"Sniff."

My eyes flew open, and I saw her whisk something away behind her back.

"You're so weird sometimes." She wandered to the back of the apartment, and I heard her in the kitchen and shouted for her to turn off the kettle. Moments later, she returned with an eye mask she occasionally wore to combat puffiness. "Put this on."

I held it like it was a rattlesnake about to strike my face.

Sarah laughed it off, and I wondered if she thought I was being playful. With the mask firmly in place, she ordered me to sniff again. I did.

"Smells good. Cinnamon apple?" I asked.

"Good." She still didn't explain the game, and I was completely clueless. "Now this one."

"Uh, Christmas," I guessed.

"Yes, it's called Christmas Memories." She sounded thrilled.

Sensing there was a new thing to smell, I inhaled deeply. "Lavender," I answered smugly. I didn't understand the point, but at least I was scoring well. *God, I'm such a nerd.*

Sarah waved three more items under my nose, and only the last one stumped me. I scratched the top of my head. "I don't know. It smells clean."

She ripped the mask off my face. "Wow! I'm impressed you know your Yankee Candles."

I tilted my head. "What?"

Instead of answering, she gestured to the tiny glass containers aligned on the coffee table, mimicking a hostess on a game show. "I picked up all these candles for the apartment. Which is your favorite?"

"The last one."

She handed it to me. "Clean cotton." I nodded. "I do like the smell of clothes fresh out of the dryer."

"Fitting — for you."

"What does that mean?" I asked, not insulted but curious.

"You're the most fastidious person I've met. Do I need to mention Miranda? Whom I've never met, by the way. Does she really exist?"

"Oh, she exists. The shine around here proves it. I've only seen her a couple of times myself. She has a key, and I leave the money on the kitchen counter."

"That surprises me." Sarah slumped down in the chair opposite the couch. "You're so guarded, yet she has a key and can come and go whenever she wants."

"Come and go? Why would she want to come here on her non-scheduled days?"

Sarah studied the bookshelves. "Good point. From the snooping I've done, you don't have any DVDs besides black-and-white flicks, your TV is ancient, and no CDs, unless you count audiobooks. You log on to your neighbor's Wi-Fi." She quirked an eyebrow. "The only type who would break in would be a neo-Nazi in search of Hitler's manifesto."

Her assessment was harsh — spot-on, but harsh. I nodded. "So, you've snooped."

"Not intentionally. One night while you were in your office, I was cooking dinner and wanted to put a CD in. I scanned your collection and saw you didn't have any music. Luckily, I had my laptop so I didn't have to cook in silence. I didn't want to interrupt my favorite workaholic." Her smile teased me.

I walked over to my CD collection. "What's wrong with this?" I tossed her a box.

Sarah read the title. "*To Kill a Mockingbird*."

"You are an English teacher, right?"

She laughed. "True. But unlike you, I like to unwind, not work or try to improve myself every waking moment."

"I don't do that."

"Really?" She stood, strode to the mantle, and pointed to the one-a-day calendar. "Define today's word." She snared the calendar. "Sinecure."

"A well-paying job that requires little work."

She flipped the page over and nodded. "Correct. Let's look at tomorrow's."

"Wait!" I shouted. I darted off the couch, snatching the calendar from her before she could utter the word. "Don't ruin the surprise." I placed the calendar next to a picture frame Sarah had purchased last week and filled with a recent photo of us.

"You are an odd one. What's a fancy word for odd?" She smiled as if she knew I couldn't resist.

"That depends on the definition. If you mean unusual, you could say *peculiar, atypical,* or *deviant.*" She shook her head playfully after I said deviant. "But if you mean *abnormal,* you have many more options: *aberrant, eccentric, heteroclite, heteromorphic, queer.*" I made a circular motion with my hand. Being this close to Sarah, I was incapable of controlling myself. I leaned in to kiss her neck and then flicked her earlobe with my tongue. She let out a soft sigh.

"Vocabulary gets you hot?" she joked.

"Yeah." I pulled back. "It doesn't work for you?" Smiling, I popped open the top button of her silk blouse and leaned down to kiss her chest as I worked to undo the rest of the buttons. "Your breasts are sublime."

"That's a fancy word for the girls."

"Really? It isn't really that fancy."

"Go on, keep talking dirty to me," Sarah murmured.

"One could say breasts this perfect are *recherché.*" I unclasped her bra and took her perfect pink nipple in my mouth.

"What does that mean?" she whispered.

"Rare."

"I see." Her chest rose and fell beneath my mouth; she was breathing so heavily.

I fell to my knees and unzipped her jeans. They slid down her slender legs and billowed around her ankles on the ground. Sarah stepped out of them and kicked them aside. I licked her satin panties, right on her sweet spot, making her sigh.

Not wanting to waste time, I tugged her underwear down, my tongue still teasing the inside of her thighs. Sarah spread her legs to give me full access.

"Seems someone is titillated." I waggled my eyebrows.

She laughed. "Who knew vocab could be hot?"

"I did, of course. It turns all the women on." I peered up to gauge her response.

Sarah navigated my head between her legs. "No more talking."

I agreed and took her lips into my mouth. Spreading them with my tongue, I explored, enjoying her taste. She let out a tiny squeal and swayed against me.

"Here." I patted the carpet in front of the fireplace. I smiled when I spied the unnecessary firewood bucket that Sarah had purchased two weekends ago. The fireplace was electric. She'd filled it with cedar scented pinecones to add a personal touch and apparently to counter the mustiness from my book collection.

Sarah yanked my head to her lips. The fire was raging now, but I felt hotter. I gazed up into Sarah's eyes. From the look on her face, three fires raged in the room.

Shucking off my sweater and T-shirt, I lay down on top of her, my right hand trailing up and down her slender body. Her hips rose, grinding into mine.

"My cooter needs you," she whispered in my ear.

I pulled up. "Cooter?"

"What? Ms. Vocab doesn't know that definition of pussy?" She ran her fingers through my hair.

I smiled. "Can't say I've heard that one before."

"What about fur pie?"

I shook my head. She grinded against my hip again.

"Poontang," she whispered as I inserted a finger, eager to be inside her. Sarah continued, "Honey pot."

I added another finger and dove in deeper. Soon, my entire hand was slick with her juices. Her back arched, and I moved up to kiss her deeply, my tongue exploring her mouth as my fingers simultaneously penetrated her. When I came up for air, Sarah panted, "One of my least favorite terms is fuckhole, but right now Lizzie, I want you to fuck me. Oh God, fuck me hard."

I plunged in as deep as I could. She was so wet. Her nails scored my back, but when I lapped her clit, both of her hands gripped my hair, holding me right where she wanted me. No teasing today. She didn't have to hold me in place. I wanted to be there — taking her into my mouth, feeling her wetness dribble down my chin. No one tasted as good as Sarah.

Her body began its pre-orgasm quiver, and my fingers and tongue worked together to carry her completely there, to that place where her nails gripped my skull and her back arced. I pushed in deeper.

"Oh fuck!" she bellowed.

I held my fingers in place.

"Oh fuck. Oh fuck. Oh fuck," she chanted. Her body shuddered for several moments before she slunk into the plush carpet. I rested my head on her still-quivering thigh. The lower half of my face was slick, but I was too spent to care.

Sarah guided me up again, my mouth to hers, relishing tasting herself. Before I knew what was happening, she had me on my back and she was tugging my jeans off. Once my panties where dispensed with, she didn't waste any time. I let out a yelp as I felt her fingers inside me.

Her mouth eagerly explored my fuckhole. Funny to think the crass term was now turning me on. The sensation between my legs proved it, or it could have been the stunning woman there. I lifted my head and watched her. Her eyes met mine, and the emotions emanating from them matched my own. How peculiar that such base acts — fingering and licking — could be the ultimate way to show someone how much you care for them.

She plunged in deeper, and all thought spilled from my

head. I teetered on the brink of orgasm, each flick of her tongue bringing me one dizzying step closer. "Jesus!" I shouted, immediately following it up with, "Don't stop."

Sarah knew how to bring me home. Her fingers quickened, and she paid attention to my clit. It pulsed with each brush of her fingertips. Not wanting to close my eyes, I forced them to stay open to watch her. I wanted to tell her I loved her, but something made me hold back.

Then it hit me. Lights danced before my eyes, and I felt them roll back, making it impossible for me to stay focused on Sarah.

Sarah.

I was falling in love with her.

How could this be?

Love and I didn't work out. Pain would inevitably follow; it always did. But I couldn't control my emotions.

An earthquake rattled through my body as Sarah stilled her tongue and fingers. After a couple of aftershocks, I lay perfectly still while she worked her way back up, tenderly kissing my body along the way. For several minutes, neither of us spoke as she nestled against me. I was thinking about love: cruel, exciting love.

"What does that frown mean?" She snaked her fingers over the creases in my brow.

I smiled and gazed into her eyes. "Fuckhole? Really?"

Chapter Fourteen

"I RAN INTO MEG THE other day." I crossed my legs.

"What's Soy Sauce Meg up to?" asked Ethan.

He wasn't referring to Meg's ethnicity. He'd nicknamed her that after an incident that occurred after we broke up. Meg had tried to use every excuse in the book to wheedle her way back into my life. At one point, she'd called to tell me she'd left some soy sauce at my place. It wasn't even a large bottle. Maybe if it had been Costco size, I would have understood. She hounded me for days until I finally told her to come by my place and get it. Not wanting to see her, I'd placed it outside my apartment door minutes before she was due to arrive.

Meg hadn't taken too kindly to that. She'd pounded on my door, insisting I open up. Luckily, my neighbor Carl walked by and asked her if there was a problem. I knew that because I was standing on the other side of the door, peering through the peephole. It was obvious she was drunk, and Carl had threatened to call the cops, which spooked Meg. She left, but she'd continued to call for several more weeks and didn't stop until she entered rehab. Now, most of our communication was done via text to set up clandestine money handoffs.

At one point, I'd slipped up and mentioned the soy sauce

incident to Ethan, but I hadn't told him I was visibly shaking while Meg was pounding on my door. Dealing with an alcoholic was not for the fainthearted. I also neglected to tell Ethan it was one of Meg's pathetic attempts to wheedle her way back into my life. Instead, I insinuated it was one of her cruel games — for me to be at her beck and call in hopes of rekindling our relationship.

"She cornered me in a public restroom."

Ethan raised an eyebrow. "I take it that didn't go well."

I shrugged. "You know Meg." I knew full well that he didn't — not completely.

He tutted. "It's a shame. She was so intelligent. Why'd she quit history altogether? She could teach."

"Oh, I think her passion ran out. For history, I mean."

Plus, it was nearly impossible to get a teaching job when you had two DUIs and a stint in rehab — and, according to Janice, looked like a prossie.

"Did Sarah see her?"

"Fortunately, no. We skedaddled pretty quickly after the bathroom incident." I hadn't told Ethan about the run-in at the Italian restaurant.

"Probably a wise move. Having exes meet is never a good thing. Both of them would probably pretend to be cool with it, but you know they'd be sizing each other up. Women can be brutal!"

"Oh, please. Haven't you met one of Lisa's exes? I'm sure you're just as brutal, if not more."

"She did have one boyfriend before me, but he died in a car accident when he was sixteen."

"Wow. That's awful. I had no idea."

Ethan scrunched his mouth around the words. "Needless to say, I never bring him up. If she does, I'm sympathetic. It's hard to compete with a dead guy."

I thought Ethan was lucky. I knew it was heartless to think like that, but it would be much easier if I didn't have to live in the same town as Meg. If she came back to school, it would be horrendous. However, the likelihood of Dr. Marcel letting her back was slim to none.

Ethan continued, "One thing that really bugs me is that Lisa's dad always praises her ex. Talks about how he was the quarterback and our high school won state because of him. He wasn't impressed that her next boyfriend" – he pointed to himself – "was an intellectual who never played a sport."

I smiled. "That makes two of us. Half the time, I'm sure people are thinking *nerd alert* whenever I walk into a room."

My comment made him laugh, easing him out of his funk. "It's probably closer to three quarters of the time." He licked his lips, deep in thought. "Whatcha going to do about Meg?"

"Ignore her to the best of my ability."

I didn't mention that I'd met up with her to hand over five hundred bucks in cash. If I thought it'd work, I'd offer her half a mill to leave town.

But I knew that even if I did that, she'd still come back with her hand out.

He flashed his knowing smile. "Ah, Sarah's good for you. In the past you would have been pining away for Meg. Progress!" He slammed down his cup. I gulped my chai. In the Meg department, the only progress being made was draining my trust fund.

AFTER COFFEE WITH Ethan, I headed over to the university library. Lately, when I wasn't with Sarah I was in my office, studying, writing lectures, or grading – or at home doing the same. The office was depressing on the weekends. Even though I was a socially awkward, self-involved loner, working in the office when no one was around felt too lonely, even for me.

Home wasn't as bad because I was surrounded by my stuff. But on days when I wanted to be alone while still being in a public place, the library was the perfect solution. People were always milling about, yet few stopped to chat, and if they did, only briefly. So, I wasn't surprised when Janice caught my eye. I waved and then suppressed a groan when she marched over and took a seat at the secluded table I'd selected because it was mostly hidden from view. The table was in the European history section, which was probably how Janice had stumbled upon me.

"Imagine finding you here," she said with a smile. Motioning to my stack, she asked, "How's your dissertation coming along?"

I nodded noncommittally. "Not bad. Yours?"

She shrugged. Janice didn't seem to be in any rush to finish. Secretly, I hated her for that. All my life I'd pushed myself to my limits. It wasn't that she wasn't intelligent — she was quite brilliant — but that her motivation was severely lacking. She knew it, and it didn't bother her one bit. Me, I was hell-bent on finishing my dissertation a year ahead of schedule. Dr. Marcel chided me about rushing, but I didn't want to stop.

"Have you seen Meg lately?" she asked, nibbling on a fingernail. This was becoming a typical conversation starter between us.

"Briefly last week. You?"

She nodded and then peeked over her shoulder to ensure we were alone. "She asked Dr. Marcel to let her back into the program."

I nodded. To keep my emotions under control, I tapped a pen against the side of the table.

Janice leaned back in her chair. "He's thinking about it, according to Meg."

"Really?" I said, not wanting to play my hand.

Her eyes bored into mine, trying to get her point across. It wasn't working. "It's surprising he's even considering it."

I smiled weakly.

"I thought you'd like to know."

"Thanks."

Janice waited for me to say more. I had no intention of doing so.

"How much this time?" she asked after a moment.

"How'd you know?"

"I can see it in your eyes. The guilt. So?"

"More than I should have."

"She got 250 from me," confessed Janice.

I whistled, giving the impression I'd given Meg less than that, not double. "She's a sieve."

"Her latest roommate kicked her out, and she said she needed first and last month's rent." Janice shrugged. "Hard to know the truth with her." She shook her head. "I miss the old Meg."

I didn't say anything.

Janice stood up, now unburdened by the secrets. "I'll let you get back to it." She pointed to my stack of books.

As if I could focus now. "Okey dokey, smokey," I said, hoping she wouldn't worry about me, even though I knew she would.

Janice flashed an odd smile, dipped her head, and then vanished around the corner.

I waited a few moments and then muttered, "Shit." I'd thought for sure Dr. Marcel would instantly refuse Meg's request. But he was thinking about it. Actually thinking about it.

Fucking hell.

Chapter Fifteen

DR. MARCEL HADN'T MENTIONED THAT Meg had approached him. Not that he was obligated to tell me, a grad student, but he'd been the first to tell me she'd been kicked out of the program. At the time, it was no secret we were a couple, so I guess Dr. Marcel wanted me to hear what really happened from him, and only him. I never told him that Meg hit me or that I'd broken it off before she showed up at the conference drunk, but I think he knew a lot more than he let on. Who knew what Meg had said to him when she was inebriated? The night I'd met him at his house after returning from the East Coast, my lip was swollen and my face showed bruising I'd attempted to cover with makeup. When he told me the news, his eyes had seemed kinder than usual.

Now, I anxiously waited to hear from him, or from Janice, about whether he had refused or accepted Meg's request.

To add another layer of stress, Sarah suddenly went MIA. Over the past week, she'd stayed at my place only on Sunday night. For four days, I received texts that offered little information, which was worrisome. On Thursday night, she knocked on my door, balancing two large pizzas.

"Come in."

"I knew you wouldn't turn down food." She kissed my cheek

as she breezed by.

"Were you afraid I wouldn't let you in?" I was somewhat peeved, surprisingly. *What happened to the woman who enjoyed her alone time?*

"I would be upset in your shoes if my girlfriend disappeared."

"Girlfriend?" I parroted.

Sarah still held the pizza boxes. "Isn't that what we are?"

"Of course," I stammered. "We just never clarified."

"I've practically been living in your apartment. What'd you think we were?"

"I guess I never stopped to contemplate our status."

"That's so like you." She shook the boxes. "Are you hungry?"

"Yes, ma'am."

After retrieving plates from the kitchen, we settled on the couch.

"How was your week?" Sarah asked as if nothing was wrong, although I gathered she was holding something back.

I shrugged. "Not much to share, really." *Oh, except my evil, blackmailing ex might be a colleague once again.* "You?"

Her bottom lip quivered.

I set my plate down. "Are you all right?"

"It's Haley."

Haley had been Sarah's roommate all throughout college.

Her behavior made me wonder whether Haley was more than an old college friend, though. Or had been in the past. I was close to Ethan, but I never fretted over him the way Sarah seemed to be doing right now over Haley, not even when he'd quit his program.

"I've been staying at her place this week," she continued.

"Oh," was all I managed.

Sarah didn't pick up on the accusation in my tone. It wasn't like we had an understanding or anything. She was free to date, and so was I. Yet, I just assumed that, like me, she didn't want to date others. Shit, I just found out our new relationship status.

"Her boyfriend is such an asshole."

A rush of relief whooshed out.

"How so?" I caressed her thigh.

"He's abusive, controlling — "

I swallowed too much air, thinking of Meg, and felt a lump in my throat. Finally, I was able to force out, "Abusive?"

Sarah's downcast eyes answered my question. She went on to explain. "Normally, he's just verbally abusive. He doesn't actually beat her up, but he trashed their apartment and terrified the hell out of Haley. The neighbors called the cops." She stared up at me. "I've been staying there because she didn't want to be alone."

My expression must have transformed my face into an enormous question mark.

"I know," Sarah said, nodding. "She isn't alone now. Michael is there."

"Is he a friend?"

The sad shake of Sarah's head was my only answer.

"She took him back." I stated needlessly.

"Haley always will, I fear. Michael has some kind of hold on her. I don't know what. And her self-esteem is non-existent."

Thoughts of Meg flashed through my mind. I could relate completely. But I didn't say anything to Sarah. I planned to take that secret to my grave. The shame was too much.

"It's just so hard to watch. Haley's not just a friend — she's like family and I love her." She looked away guiltily. "I'm not one to judge, but ..."

"What?" I managed to force out the question.

"I don't get it. How she can let Michael treat her that way? Does she have no shame?"

My gut told me Haley had more than enough shame to fill all the oceans in the world, but how could a strong woman like Sarah understand that. When someone beats you down, it becomes your new norm.

Sarah let out a long, cleansing breath and wiggled her arms as if trying to shake off the bad vibe.

I hated seeing her upset. "What can I do to help?"

"Know anyone" — she made a gun with her hand and cocked it at her forehead — "who can take care of it?"

I had to smile. "Can't say I do. Unless Dr. Marcel is a former CIA agent."

That made her laugh. "Oh, wouldn't that be neat! No one would ever suspect such a pleasant man of being a trained assassin. Actually, you'd make a great agent."

"Really? Why is that?" I picked up my slice of pepperoni pizza.

"I have a feeling there's much I haven't learned about you. No one can study that much." She jabbed her elbow into my side.

"You're forgetting my secret bike rides. That's when I meet my contact. On the wooden bridge by the red farmhouse."

"Do you pass notes?"

"Yes, in code. But now that you know, I'll have to kill you."

"Do I get a last request?"

"Depends on the request."

"Take me to bed."

I was mid-bite, but I instantly removed the pizza from my mouth and tossed it back on the plate.

"You did miss me this week." Her voice was velvety.

I extended my hand to help her off the couch. "Let me show you how much."

"Maybe I should spend more time away, if this is how you'll greet me."

I almost said, *please don't.*

What the hell was wrong with me?

AT MIDNIGHT THE following evening, there was a knock on my front door. Fear surged through me. I remained at my desk with a stack of exam papers and listened for a moment. Then I took a sip of my steaming hot tea, instantly regretting it — too hot. I was waving a hand frantically in front of my face to cool my tongue when I heard another knock. My hopes that someone had accidentally knocked on my door were squashed. Was it Meg?

Sarah was in Denver with her mom for some event, so I wasn't expecting to see her until tomorrow.

I cautiously checked the peephole. Sarah's head looked ginormous through the carnival-like glass. I laughed with relief.

"Why are you laughing? Open the door." She put her hands on her hips, distorting the image more.

"You looked funny," I said, opening the door.

Sarah cocked her head. "Excuse me."

That was when I noticed she was dolled up for a night on the town. "No, not that. Through the peephole you looked funny. But now ..." I motioned to her plunging red dress, stockings, and high heels. "You look amazing. Simply stunning."

That put a sexy smile on her face. "Good. Let me in." She pushed past me. "I hope you have the fire going. I'm freezing."

"I don't, but that can be corrected." I switched on the fireplace. "So, why are you dressed up?"

"Do you like it?"

The way my staring eyes devoured her should have been answer enough, but I sensed she was fishing. Instead of replying, I pulled her into my arms and kissed her. She responded passionately.

"Warmer?" I asked when we separated.

She nodded, and her hooded eyes suggested the night was only beginning.

"So, did you dress up for me?"

Sarah laughed. "Not really," she confessed, with the most adorable smile. "It was opening night for *The Magic Flute*. Mom and I enjoy the opera."

Shit, I'd never been to the opera, but if Sarah dressed up like this, I considered getting season tickets to the opera in all major surrounding cities. Did they have opera in Cheyenne?

"I've never been," I said finally, realizing I was ogling her — not that she minded.

"I'll take you sometime." She removed her thin, shiny black coat and rubbed her arms in front of the fire.

"Would you like some tea or hot chocolate?"

"Hot chocolate, please. I didn't realize how cold it would be tonight. When is spring officially going to arrive?" She motioned to her jacket, which was more for show than for warmth.

"Be back in a jiffy. I just made a cup of tea, so the kettle should still be warm."

By the time I returned, Sarah had stripped off her dress. She pirouetted around from the fireside, and I almost spilled the hot chocolate when I saw her black-lace cami and garter. She still wore her four-inch stilettos, too. She looked sexier than any *Victoria's Secret* model — not that I perused those kind of magazines frequently, not since high school, at least.

She slunk toward me and plucked the cup from my hand. "You okay?" Her smirk implied she knew exactly what thoughts were racing through my mind.

"I think I've died and gone to heaven," was all I could think of to say.

"I love it when you get all flustered. I thought about texting to warn you, but decided to surprise you instead."

"And what a wonderful surprise. Much better than grading."

"Is that why you're still up? Poor thing. I can go to bed and leave you alone." Her smile said she would, but her eyes indicated she didn't want to go to bed alone.

"Not necessary. I have 'til Monday."

"We can work together on Sunday. I have essays to read." She inhaled the steam from the cup. "Ah, thanks. This is helping."

I watched Sarah sip her hot chocolate, swirling a dissipating marshmallow with her finger. She stood with her back to me, warming herself in front of the fire. Her head pivoted, and she motioned me hither with a jerk of her neck.

She set her cup on the mantle. Smiling like a fool, I rushed to embrace her.

"I was wondering how long you were going to make me wait. Decided it would be easier for me to get the ball rolling," she said.

"I was enjoying the view. One word: A-maz-ing. I'll never think of hot chocolate the same way."

She melted against me. "Sometimes you say the sweetest things."

I peppered her neck with kisses. "I love the way you smell." I sniffed. "Vanilla and gardenia?"

She nodded. I smoothed my hands down her body and traced them back up, unembarrassed by the moan of desire that escaped my lips.

"Take me to bed. I've been waiting all night," she whispered.

All night? I'd been waiting for a woman like Sarah all my life.

"YOU KNOW" – SARAH rolled over in bed – "if I had a key, I could pop in like this more often and surprise you. How would you like me to wake you up in the middle of the night – naked?"

I whimpered, satisfied. Turning my head on the pillow, I

replied, "I'd like that a lot."

"Why'd it take you so long to answer the door earlier?" She flicked a strand of mussed hair out of my eyes.

"Er ..." *Quick, Lizzie, think of something plausible.* "I thought someone had knocked on my door accidentally."

Sarah searched my eyes before saying, "What? You don't get a lot of visitors?" She feigned mock surprise.

"Not on the weekends. The women of the night only visit Monday through Thursday."

"The women of the night," she chortled. "Is that how you think of me?"

Ignoring her question, I asked, "How often do you wear that lace thing?"

"I bought it last weekend, just for tonight."

"For the opera?"

"For you."

"I've never liked shopping, but the next time you go" – I motioned to her lingerie on the floor – "sign me up. I'm buying everything you want."

"What I want? I'm pretty sure you'll want it more." She trailed one finger over my lips.

"Most definitely."

"You're on. I'm going shopping with my mom tomorrow – "

"You bought that with your mom watching? And you want me to join both of you?" I couldn't hide my shock.

"Of course not," she laughed. "If you'd let me finish ... I was going to say that Mom has lunch plans, so you can meet me in Denver for lunch and some shopping of our own tomorrow afternoon."

"Deal." I made her shake on it, much to her delight. Then I glanced at the digital clock radio on my nightstand. It was after three. "Shall we get some sleep?"

"Not yet."

I cupped her chin. "I could never get enough of you, not even in the early hours."

Her eyes beckoned, and her soft lips welcomed me back. "I hope not," she whispered.

Chapter Sixteen

THE NEXT DAY, I EAGERLY stepped into the trendy Tex-Mex restaurant. Neither of us had slept much, but it didn't matter. Images of Sarah, posing before my fireplace in her black-lace garter slip and stilettos danced before my eyes and made me giddy. I closed them to cherish the memory of freeing her from her lingerie, slowly rolling the stockings down her slender legs ... pure heaven.

"Can I help you?" asked the hostess.

My eyes snapped open to see the most insufferable forced smile.

"Yes, I'm meeting someone for lunch. The name is Cavanaugh."

The woman beamed. "Oh, you must be Lizzie. I've heard all about you."

I staggered backward, feeling trapped in an *Alfred Hitchcock Presents* episode. "Is she here?"

"Yep. Both of them."

Both?

The hostess looped her arm through mine and led me through the maze of tables, snaking our way through the massive dimly-lit restaurant. Every table was occupied, and the place buzzed with chatter, laughter, clinking glasses, and country music over the speakers. She patted my arm. "Sarah is such a lovely woman. You better behave — if you get my drift." She let out an obnoxious giggle that made her sound like a chipmunk. "Only kidding, of course." But the vise-like grip on my arm said otherwise. What was this place? A lesbian mafia hangout?

I spied Sarah in the back, seated at the best table in the joint. A woman sat with her, but I could only see the back of her head. Noticing me, Sarah waved, and her companion slowly turned. I nearly swallowed my own tongue! She could have been Sarah's twin, only twenty years or more older.

Sarah's mom.

I was having lunch with Sarah and her mom.

If there'd been a panic button in sight, I would have slammed it several times with my forehead!

"Here's Lizzie." The demented woman added six e's to the end of my name.

Sarah stood, brushed my cheek with hers, and gently forced me down into the seat next to her. I was pretty sure she realized I was going into panic mode. My autopilot, which usually took over in such situations, also seemed to be malfunctioning. It would be a miracle if I didn't have spittle oozing down my chin and resemble a stroke victim.

"Lizzie, I'd like you to officially meet my mom, Rose."

Rose nodded, eyeing me.

Sarah kicked my shin under the table.

"It's very nice to meet you, Rose," I said as pleasantly as possible. My tone was robotic, and my body movements matched it. My best hope was that I resembled C-3PO from *Star Wars*. At least he had a certain charm that millions of people adored. I needed Rose to like me just a smidgen, so I could continue sleeping with her smoking-hot daughter.

"Mom's friend cancelled," Sarah said too breezily, giving me the impression I'd been played. Had she and her mom cooked up this plan at the opera last night?

Yes, they had. I could see it in Sarah's eyes.

"Of course, she can't stay for our shopping excursion." Sarah's tone was neutral and not overly seductive, but I got her meaning: play nice and you'll be rewarded later.

"I'm so sorry to hear about your friend canceling," I said. "But hey, it worked out for me. Sarah has told me so much about you."

I could see the tension slipping out of Sarah's body.

Rose sipped her water. "So, Sarah tells me you're a college professor. That's impressive for someone your age."

I cleared my throat. "Actually, I'm a PhD student, but I teach Western Civ classes as part of my scholarship."

"Scholarship. Sarah received a full ride at CU. Not that she needed it."

Did Rose have money? Or was she the responsible type that had started a college fund before Sarah was walking?

Rose picked up her menu. "I recommend the enchiladas. You aren't a vegetarian, are you?"

I shook my head. If I were, I would have lied anyway.

"Great." She snapped her fingers, and a waiter magically appeared. "Ricky, can we start with queso verduras and ceviche? Then I think we'll all get the lobster enchiladas."

"Excellent choices, Rose."

Sarah flinched, but said nothing. I quickly scanned the starters, identifying that queso verduras were sautéed green peppers, mushrooms, and onions. Ceviche was seafood-based. Basically, Rose had just requested everything on the menu that I normally wouldn't touch with a ten-foot pole.

Ricky yanked the menu from my fingers without giving me a

chance to amend the order.

"Oh, and three Big Tex Margaritas," Rose added.

"Mom, I'm not sure Lizzie can drink this early."

"Pfffft. From what I saw that night, she enjoys a drink," Rose said in such a friendly, confident way that it even convinced me I could handle the alcohol.

Sarah's tight-lipped smile was adorable.

"Oh, there's John, the owner. I need to say hi." Rose disappeared into the lunch crowd.

Sarah nudged my arm. "I'm sorry, she can be a bit much. But she enjoys showing off, and I think she likes you."

"How can you tell?"

"She's putting on a show ... more than normal." Sarah leaned her head against mine. "Mom is trying hard to impress you."

"Shouldn't it be the other way around?" I whispered.

Sarah patted my leg. "It's good to see you. I missed you."

That made me laugh. We'd only been apart for a few hours. "Everyone here seems to know you two."

"We've been having lunch here every Saturday for as long as I can remember. It's a family-owned establishment, and we've become an unofficial part of the group over the years."

"You come to Denver every Saturday?"

"The shopping's better here." She gave me her *duh* look.

"But every weekend?"

"I know. Many people assume that women who love to shop are empty-headed bimbos. But we like it and we're good at it, so why not enjoy it? Many of our friends have asked us to help them snazz up their homes or wardrobes. I know a certain someone who's started to dress better."

She eyed my outfit and feigned disgust. I wasn't wearing anything she'd purchased for me recently.

"Dr. Marcel complimented my work outfit on Friday." I tugged on my silver hoop earring. I still wasn't used to the accessory, but it reminded me of Sarah.

"And your apartment isn't as sterile."

True, but she neglected to mention that I hadn't asked for help.

"Mom and I love to shop for other people. Earlier we were buying birthday gifts for my friend's son. The father was recently laid off," she explained. "Every Christmas we adopt several families who can't afford gifts and we go hog wild – a real tree, full turkey dinner, and gifts coming out of the wazoo. No child should have to go without Christmas gifts."

"Oh. That's nice." Sarah didn't have a car, but she was buying gifts for poor people and clothes for me? This wasn't adding up. I knew she had a heart of gold with all her school activities and Haley, but she needed to learn to take care of herself.

Rose ambled back, and all of our attention swiveled to her. I guessed it was always like that with Rose, no matter where she went. She reminded me a little of the Unsinkable Molly Brown, but with a bit more class.

"How do you like being a grad student?"

Let the interrogation begin.

"I love it, actually. I know a lot of people don't find history very exciting, but I love research."

"You should see her apartment, Mom. She has books everywhere."

"What time period do you study?" Rose's eyes were so much like Sarah's I found it unnerving.

"Twentieth-century European history. My concentration is on World War II, focusing on the Hitler Youth."

"Ah, the German Boy Scouts." She threw it out there

casually, but the slight smile on Sarah's face told me she had already filled her mom in on my specialty subject. Rose *was* trying to impress me; this was new. Parents, mothers especially, usually didn't like me.

"How have you been able to afford so much schooling?"

Sarah's eyes widened, but she didn't interfere.

Her question put me in an awkward spot — not because I was poor, the opposite in fact, but because I feared telling people I was a trust-fund baby. I weighed my options. Admit it and impress Rose, but how would Sarah react? Would Sarah treat me differently if she knew the truth? I decided to deflect.

"I'm fortunate. Not only do I have a scholarship, but they actually provide a small teaching stipend. Luckily, I don't require much."

"Except for a housecleaner and having your groceries delivered." Sarah's eyes twinkled. She seemed to be enjoying watching me in the hot seat.

"Ah, necessities. At least the groceries, or I'd starve." I winked at Sarah, who slid her hand up my thigh under the table. I yanked on my collar and cleared my throat.

"Nothing wrong with spoiling yourself a little. I imagine you have your hands full with your studies." Rose looked around the crowded restaurant. "Finally," she said as the waiter set down our drinks.

"I'm so sorry, Rose. The bartender is swamped, but he did add something special to yours."

Rose smiled and took a sip. "Oh, this is marvelous!" She gave it a sizable swig.

With trepidation, I tasted mine. I imagined my eyebrow hairs boinging straight up from my forehead. So much tequila! Willing the tears out of my eyes, I said, "Yum."

The waiter left happy. Sarah eyeballed me, concerned —

especially once she sampled hers. I couldn't blame her. I was her ride home, and if I drank even half of this drink, I'd be drunker than drunk.

"You seem like a thinker." Rose placed one hand on the table, her fingers splayed, drumming. "James, her father, was the scholarly type. His health prevented him from pursuing all the degrees he wanted, but James always had a nose in a book. It's nice to see our daughter finally dating someone with some brains. Don't get me started on that one ex of yours, Sarah."

Sarah rolled her eyes for my benefit.

Rose noticed and shook a finger in Sarah's direction and then leaned over conspiratorially. "I should warn you, once she decides she wants something, she doesn't stop until she gets it." Rose let out an intimidating bark of laughter.

Turning to Sarah, I saw she wasn't upset at all by her mother's comments. She was proud.

I knocked back a third swig of the margarita, regretting it instantly as the burning liquid tried to force its way back up my throat. I swallowed, doing my best to hide my discomfort, although I was fairly certain Sarah had picked up on it.

Rose spun around to her daughter. "You see? She loves her drink." She snapped her fingers at the waiter, indicating we wanted another round. This was going to be a long, excruciatingly boozy lunch.

"Oh, there's Milton." With that, she stood again and chased after a man walking the other way.

"She's a social butterfly," I said and then burped.

Sarah swapped my drink with hers, which was almost empty. How was it possible that both of their drinks were nearly finished? Sarah didn't seem fazed at all, which impressed me. She poured water into my new margarita glass instead. The glass wasn't clear — fortunately for the ruse.

"Thanks," I said, avoiding her eyes.

She reached out and stroked my cheek. "I can't have you passing out before we get our shopping done. Of course, I'll have to try everything on for you when we get back."

I nodded, appreciating that she was willing to ignore my inability to hold my liquor. "Your mom seems friendly." I scouted over my shoulder to see Rose chatting with several people at the bar across the room.

"Oh, she's a sweetheart." Sarah cut her eyes upward. "Unless, of course, you piss her off. She doesn't forgive easily."

Was she speaking from personal experience, or was that a warning? I didn't have time to find out.

By the time dessert arrived, I was slightly tipsy. Whenever Rose excused herself to chat or visit the bathroom, Sarah did her best to get rid of my latest drink by continually swapping her nearly empty glass with my almost full one. I'd barely touched my enchiladas, too. Lobsters belonged in the ocean, not in an enchilada. When it came to seafood, I could only stomach shrimp, and usually only if it was fried. As soon as the waiter placed my crispy sopapilla with vanilla ice cream and cinnamon and sugar in front of me, I dug in hungrily. Sarah spoon-fed me several bites of her flan, too, and I didn't refuse.

"Shall we have a shot for the road?" Rose asked. It was clear she was already blotto.

"Mom. You have to drive!" Sarah wasn't playing nice anymore. I have to admit I was impressed by how well both of them held their liquor.

Rose waved her off. "Ricky arranged a car for me."

Sarah looked relieved, but her eyes implored me to say no to the shot. I wanted to. But how did I say no to Rose? The woman scared the crap out of me.

When Ricky arrived with the check, Sarah rushed to thank

him before Rose had time to order anything else.

AT AROUND TWO in the afternoon, we finally made it to the lingerie store.

"What is this?" I held up a sexy, lacy red item.

Sarah giggled at my lingerie incompetence. "It's a bustier."

"What does it do?" I whispered.

"Technically, it pushes your bust up by squeezing your midriff," she whispered back.

"And not technically?"

"It turns your partner on."

I nodded, admiring the scarlet contraption. "Will you try it on?"

Sarah glanced around, taking in the scene surreptitiously. No one was near the dressing rooms, and only one door was ajar. I was okay with holding hands and such in public, but sharing a dressing room in a lingerie store was pushing my lesbian comfort zone. Today, no one would be the wiser.

Sarah entered the room, holding several pairs of bras and panties we'd selected together. I followed, gripping the bustier.

Sarah removed her coat, and I helped her take off her sweater and T-shirt. Encircling her, I unhooked her bra, letting my hands linger on her creamy skin.

She slipped out of her jeans. "Just for you, since I won't be trying on the panties," she said, hooking on the first bra. She knew I wanted to see the bustier, but I had a feeling that would be dessert.

The night-sky bra with green embroidery pushed her tits upward in a way that made my breath hitch. Sarah raised an eyebrow, and I nodded approvingly. She held up the matching panties. I was sure the look in my eyes insisted that buying both was a must — an absolute must.

We went through the same routine for all the bras, with me nodding enthusiastically for each and every one. Who knew shopping could be this entertaining?

Finally, she laced up the bustier. Until then, I had been a good girl, but now I couldn't stop myself. Taking her in my arms, I kissed her. Sarah's mouth welcomed my own, her tongue frantically meeting mine. Just when I was working up the courage to take it further, someone coughed outside the dressing room door. Both Sarah and I stifled a laugh. Could the person see two pairs of legs under the wooden door that obnoxiously stopped a foot above the ground?

"I have a plan. Get dressed," I commanded. Sarah didn't seem aggravated by my bossiness. She dressed hurriedly while I gathered all of the merchandise and marched up to the register.

A perky twenty-something woman with dyed blonde hair asked, "Did you find everything all right?"

I couldn't peel my eyes off her dark roots. "Yes. Thank you."

Sarah sidled up to me, and her proximity sent me in a dither.

I wasn't sure if Miss Perky had noticed the sexual tension, but she quickly rang up our purchases and I whipped out my American Express card before Sarah had time to think of reaching for her purse.

Sarah's expression told me she had registered my Amex. I hoped she hadn't noticed it was a platinum card, not the everyday blue.

"Wow. Grad students don't do so badly after all," she muttered with an odd expression on her face.

"I deliver newspapers in the morning on my bike," I joked, keeping my tone light. After completing the transaction, I whisked Sarah out of the store, doing my best to ignore the stab of regret for not telling her the truth about my finances.

"What's your plan?" She seemed calm, her voice soothing

but still with a sexual tinge.

I motioned to a bookshop on the corner, the lingerie bag swinging from my arm as I gestured for Sarah to walk ahead of me.

"Books? Somehow I thought you planned to do something else." She ran a slender finger along my jawline before stepping ahead of me.

"Okay, can you entertain yourself for ten minutes? Twenty tops."

"Wait. You're abandoning me?"

"If I take you, it won't be a surprise." I planted a kiss on top of her head.

Sarah pursed her lips, and I could tell she was excited and irked in equal measure at being kept out of the loop.

"Trust me," I said before I disappeared, rushing back to the mall. I needed to get a couple of things. The perky sales assistant in the lingerie shop recognized me and buzzed over to me like a moth to a flame.

"Did you forget something?" Her overly sweet tone made me wonder if she worked on commission.

"Yes." I marched over to a satin kimono. "The woman who was with me earlier — what size do you think would fit her?" I noticed Sarah eyeing it earlier, but, with a look of regret, she'd said it was too much.

The fake blonde searched through their supply. "Ah, I think this one."

"Fantastic. Do you wrap gifts?"

She nodded as she led me to the register.

At the counter, I added a selection of bubble baths. "Can you recommend anything?" I nodded to the selection of perfume and lotions behind the counter.

"Of course." She set out several fragrances and lotions, and

I gestured that I'd take it all.

"I'll be back in a few moments," I told her as I paid. "Can you please wrap everything?"

My next stop was a luggage store.

I checked my watch. Ten minutes had passed. Around the corner of Sixteenth Street Mall was one of Denver's swankiest hotels. I rushed in, contemplating the lobby — the marble floors, the *Gone with the Wind* staircase, the elegant vases of white flowers, and all the wall sconces. It definitely made an impression. The clerk, a skinny man with an overly manicured goatee, said, "Can I help you?"

"Do you have a room available?"

"For tonight?" The corners of his mouth curled up.

"Yes. For tonight."

"I'm not sure." He clicked on the computer mouse, frowning at the screen. "Ah, you're in luck. We have one room left."

One room ... my ass. The lobby was nearly empty. Pompous prick.

"Fantastic. I'll take it."

"It's one of our most expensive rooms," he said, his elitist air suggesting it was out of my price range. I'm guessing my T-shirt, Columbia jacket, and Gap jeans weren't the normal attire here.

I whipped out my Amex. "Can you have a chilled bottle of Champagne and flowers in the room, maybe some rose petals on the bed? And would it be possible to have this delivered to the room?" I motioned to the suitcase I'd stuffed the lingerie bag and other gifts in.

The expression that crossed his face was just short of creepy. "Of course, Madame." His attempt to sound French was laughable.

Ma-dame. Pa-lease.

"Thanks. Also, can you recommend a romantic restaurant

near here?"

The Francophile pulled out a map of the area and circled a French restaurant two blocks from the hotel.

"Perfect. My companion is fluent." I thanked him and marched toward the exit.

"Do you require a cab?" The doorman opened the door for me.

Shaking my head, I thanked him anyway.

Sarah was just finishing up at the register. I sighed. I should have known better than to leave her in a store. The woman didn't understand the word browse. "There you are," she said.

"Sorry it took so long."

She motioned for me to come outside. Curious, I followed. After she'd made sure the coast was clear, she revealed the book she'd purchased: *Lesbian Sex 101*.

"Are you trying to tell me something?" I tried to sound breezy, but my tone was tinged with worry.

"Trust me, you don't have to worry. I just thought it'd be fun."

Relieved, I said, "It does go with our earlier purchase." *And my plans for later tonight.*

"Exactly!"

Sarah gazed at my empty hands and sighed. I knew getting her the kimono was the right idea, but of course I had no idea she'd buy me one right away. "Are you ready?" I asked, hiding my smile.

"Where are we going?"

"An early dinner. I'm starving."

"I knew lobster would be too much for my sandwich lover."

"Sandwich lover – is that a position in the book you purchased?" I attempted to open the bag.

Sarah swatted me away. "You have to wait and see."

"Sounds promising."

"What restaurant were you thinking?"

"The concierge recommended one."

Sarah stopped in her tracks. "Concierge?"

"Thought it'd be nice to stay the night. Unless you don't want to."

She squealed.

"I'm hoping to hear more squealing later tonight."

"With all the lingerie and book, I think that's a definite."

I WOKE IN the middle of the night, realizing Sarah wasn't in the king-sized bed. Groggily, I wiped the tiredness from my eyes and sat up.

"I'm sorry. I didn't mean to wake you," she said from a chair across the room.

I blinked several times to clear the fog from my contacts; normally, I took them out before I went to sleep. I blinked again when I noticed she was wearing only the kimono. It draped over one leg, providing me with a wonderful view.

"Everything okay?" I asked as I positioned some pillows against the headrest, sensing she needed to talk.

"I'm just thinking."

"About?"

She waved a hand. "All this is too much."

"The room? Do you want to switch hotels?" It was more posh than my usual style. If Sarah hadn't been with me, I would be in a Best Western or something along those lines.

She laughed, but it sounded sad. "You don't have to do all this."

"All what?"

"The lingerie, the French restaurant, and now this." She motioned to the empty Champagne bottle, to the room. "How much did this cost you?"

I was relieved Ethan wasn't present. He would be snickering *I told you so.*

"It wasn't that much."

She boosted one eyebrow. "I'm not an idiot."

"I'm not implying you are. I'm just saying don't worry about my finances."

"Why? Because you have a secret stash of cash?"

I looked away and shrugged.

"Do you?" Her tone switched from accusatory to hopeful.

I nodded, not sure I wanted to confess completely. I'd assumed she would wonder how I was affording everything, but hoped she wouldn't put me on the spot. I should have known better. Sarah was much more direct than I was.

"Please, be honest with me."

I met her eyes. "I have a trust fund," I muttered.

Sarah cupped her ear. "Did I hear that right? You have a trust fund?"

"Yes," I said quietly.

Sarah burst into laughter. "This is perfect. I've been hiding mine and so have you."

"Hiding what?"

"Except for our first date, when my car actually did break down, I've had a car. I just didn't want to pick you up in the brand-spanking new Mercedes Mom insisted on buying me as an early Christmas gift."

"So, you have money?" I perked up.

"As Mom likes to say, more than God." Sarah rolled her eyes.

"Ethan says the same about me."

"Really?"

"Loads. People hate me for it."

"Me too! That's why I hid it. But why the Camry with the

missing hubcap?"

"I wasn't lying earlier when I said I had a newspaper route. I don't anymore, but during my undergrad days I did. I saved all the money to buy my own car. It felt good to buy something with my earnings for once. You know what I mean? And I don't know ... I kinda like the missing hubcap. It would bug the shit out of my mother."

Sarah giggled. "I get it. That's why I live in a shitty apartment in Loveland. I hate touching my trust fund. I live on my teacher's salary 90 percent of the time, not including the shopping, of course. My old car was in even worse shape than yours. Mom called it the coffin — the brakes were that bad. She insisted I accept her gift because she knew that otherwise I'd buy another used car."

"But what about all the times you needed a *lift* to work?" I made quote marks in the air.

Sarah shrugged. "I liked spending extra time with you in the mornings."

"So those late nights you popped over, you drove? I always felt uncomfortable that your mom knew you were shacking up with me."

She chortled. "Shacking up! You crack me up."

I smiled. "What are the odds?"

"That two lesbians in northern Colorado have trust funds?" She tittered. "This is such a relief." She leaned back in her chair. "My past girlfriends have either taken advantage of it or despised it. I could never find a happy medium in the dating world." She wrapped the kimono more snugly around her. "I'm glad I don't have to feel guilty about this."

"You like it?"

"I love it!"

"Do you hide your trust fund from everyone?" I asked.

"Mostly. Haley knows, of course."

"What about the people you buy clothes and stuff for?"

"Oh, they pay me back. What about you?"

"Of course I can pay you back." I reached for my wallet on the end table.

"Not that, silly. Who knows about your trust fund?"

"Ethan knows." And Meg-the-Blackmailer.

"What about the wicked ex?"

I had to stop and think if I said Meg's name aloud. I was fairly positive I hadn't. Shit. This wasn't a path I wanted to wander down at this time of night. Or ever. "Eventually she figured it out."

"Too many extravagant hotels?" Sarah teased.

I shrugged. "What ex of yours took advantage of you?"

Sarah snorted. "Two did, but the worst one was my last serious relationship. Kerry thought she'd hit pay dirt. We dated for a couple of years, and after six months of staying at my place every night she confessed she broke her lease and quit her job."

"You're kidding!"

"Nope. We hadn't even discussed officially moving in together or anything. When my mom found out, she hit the roof! Let's just say Kerry was out of my apartment within the week."

"Did Rose escort her out?" I laughed and shook at the same time.

"Oh, she wanted to. But no. I handled it."

"What'd Kerry do with her stuff? Didn't you notice an extra TV or something in your apartment?"

"She had a furnished apartment and sold everything but her clothes."

"A furnished apartment?" I couldn't stop an involuntary shudder.

"And you thought my place was disgusting." Sarah winked.

"I never said that."

"It was pretty clear when I found you hovering over the toilet."

I shrugged and flashed an apologetic smile.

Sarah tilted her head. "You don't talk about exes ever. How many do you have?"

"Not a lot. A couple of short-lived flings in my undergrad days, but most didn't like the fact that I studied so much, even on Friday nights. Then the one — the big one that crashed and burned not so long ago."

"She broke your heart, didn't she?"

And then some. "You could say that."

"I wondered."

"You wondered if I'm nursing a broken heart?" I asked, unsure if I wanted to hear the full answer.

"You're so guarded. It's okay. Everyone has scars."

The image was more on target than Sarah intended.

Sarah eyed me, concerned. "I don't plan on breaking your heart, Lizzie."

"What do you plan on?"

"Loving you."

I wanted so much to let her. "I hope so."

In six long strides, Sarah made it to the bed and then straddled me. I opened the kimono completely and pressed her skin against mine. Her kiss was more than a kiss — so deep it felt as if she was letting me penetrate her life completely. For the moment, I wanted to let her sink just as deeply into mine.

WE WOKE LATE the following morning, after nine. I was usually an early riser, but it's hard to wake at six when after only falling asleep at four. After the night's revelations, we'd celebrated by making love until we couldn't stay awake any longer.

"You hungry?" Sarah rested her head on one hand and outlined random shapes on my chest with the other.

"Famished." I tilted her chin to bring her face to mine and kissed her deeply. Even all the kisses we'd shared last night hadn't satiated my thirst for her.

She slapped me away. "I was talking about actual food."

"I had a feeling, but it was worth a shot." I stroked my fingers through her dark, silken hair.

She beamed. "I feel the same. But I know I need food. And if I do, you're probably even more desperate."

I nodded. My pills were keeping my thyroid levels controlled, but I still felt starved almost every second of the day. "What's our plan today?"

"What? You don't have today mapped out?" She used her bedroom voice.

"I did extend our reservation, but it's your turn to plan. I'm exhausted from yesterday. Usually, my days are the same — wake up, school, study, research, bed." I ticked each off on a finger.

"You poor dear. Are you sure you even want to get out of bed today?"

I rolled her onto her back and climbed on top. "Now that's an idea. We can try mastering some more positions." I thrust my chin toward the book on the floor.

"Don't worry. That's on the agenda. But first, breakfast," she said as she shoved me off.

AN HOUR LATER, we stepped off the elevator into the lobby.

"Wait here, I'm going to ask about a place to eat." Sarah strutted to the concierge.

I leaned against a marble column. The elevator pinged obnoxiously behind me. A corpulent man stuffed into an expensive suit escorted a woman on each arm into the center of the lobby.

Everyone stopped what they were doing to appraise the situation. It was clear the women were hookers, and the three of them were sloshed even though it was morning.

Sarah's jaw dropped as if she'd never seen prostitutes before. Her intense stare forced me to take another glance at the obnoxious trio.

Meg!

Her hair was bottle-blonde again now, and she wore makeup befitting a hooker. She was thinner, too, almost scrawny, but I still recognized her. *Just having fun and making ends meet* — I suddenly remembered the comment she'd made just weeks ago. *No way!*

Her green eyes relished the look of shock on my face. She turned them on Sarah with such a look of glee I wanted to shove her back into the elevator and hit a magic button that shot her out of the building. Luckily, Sarah seemed to have not recognized her.

Breaking free from the man's chubby fingers and arm, Meg tottered toward me.

"What the hell are you doing?" I asked as Sarah rushed to my aid.

"What I have to," Meg said, her voice slurred. "It's not like you left me much choice."

"Me?" I slammed my palm into my chest, almost knocking the breath right out. "You're blaming *me*? For *this*." I pointed to the fat man.

Meg jabbed a finger in my face. "You ruined me," she spat, venom in her tone.

"Stop blaming me. Just fucking stop."

Sarah's sharp intake of air reminded me she was witnessing one of my blowouts with Meg.

I seized Meg's arm and pulled her off to the side.

"Get your fucking hand off me." Meg shoved me.

"I'm taking you home."

Meg crossed her arms. "It doesn't work that way. You can't ruin my life and then act like you care."

"I had no idea that you resorted to ... this!" I shouted.

"If you had, would you have given me more? The small amounts you pay me here and there don't go far. You wouldn't give a damn if I offed myself. In fact, you'd probably buy the gun, wouldn't you?" Meg screamed, fingers to her forehead, mimicking blowing her brains out.

I glanced over my shoulder at Sarah, mortified she had a front seat to this charade. The confusion in her eyes forced the anger right out of my head. This wasn't the time. It wasn't the place.

A gray-haired man, flanked by an imposing, tall man in an ill-made suit approached. I assumed the more put-together man was the manager.

Meg peered frantically around the lobby. "Shit. He's gone."

"Who's gone?" I asked.

"My paycheck for the week! He hasn't paid yet."

"What? You don't ask for payment up front? You disgust me."

"I disgust you! What about you, Miss Perfect? You have all the money in the world and yet you'd let me starve. If it wasn't for you, I'd be finishing up my doctorate and would have a promising career ahead of me." She pounded both fists into my chest. "It's all your fault!" She staggered back. "I've been kind so far, but I'll destroy you."

"Ladies," the gray-haired man spread his hands wide. "Can I help you resolve your issue peacefully?"

Fortunately, the morning rush of people checking out must have filtered out earlier and only a handful of people in the lobby, including the snobby concierge, stared at us with slack jaws.

"She stole my money." Meg jerked her head in my direction.

"I did no such thing." I defended.

"I'm out two thousand because of you."

I seethed. "Not my problem. You are not my problem. I paid for your rehab and look how that worked out."

Meg shouted over my shoulder in Sarah's direction. "Real nice. I threaten to kill myself and you refuse to help me. I can't pay my rent. Can't eat. I can't go on like this." She clutched my shirt with shaking, black-nail-polished hands.

I'd seen Meg put on shows before, but this was quickly turning into her finest performance.

Before I could say a word, Sarah was at my side with all the color drained from her face. "Give her the money," she whispered.

The manager and the bruiser in a suit yanked Meg toward a back room. Meg looked at Sarah and started to say something, but the imposing man clapped a fleshy hand over her mouth.

"Lizzie, you have to help her," Sarah pleaded.

"What? Why?" I shook my head. "No, I'm done with her." I mimicked wiping my hands clean.

"Done with her? How can you say such a thing? She obviously needs help. Serious help."

"Tell me about it."

Sarah took a step back. "Then why won't you help her?" The pleading in her tone tore me up inside.

"You don't understand. I've done all I can for her."

"For her? Who the hell is she?"

"Uh ..."

"Tell me right now, or I'm leaving and not coming back."

"Sarah — "

"What's her name?" Each word was said with force.

"Can we talk about this outside?" I tugged on her arm, but Sarah shook me off.

She was dead set not leaving Meg behind.

"She's ... a ... She's Miranda!"

"Your cleaning lady is a hot prostitute?"

"I didn't know she was a prostitute until today," I countered loudly.

"Well, you can't leave her here with them."

I puffed out my cheeks, slowly releasing the pressure. "What do you suggest I do?"

"Save her."

"I've tried. Repeatedly. You've got to believe me." This much was true. But I couldn't confess it all. Not even to kind loving Sarah. If I told her about Meg, I'd have to tell her everything and I swore to myself I'd take that shame to my grave. Letting her in about the trust fund was easy compared to exposing the truth about my relationship with Meg. Show her how weak I'd been? How would Sarah ever respect Punching-Bag-Lizzie ever again?

Sarah's eyes blazed. "I don't even know who I'm talking to right now, Lizzie." She spun around and headed for the door.

I had to stop her. God knows what Meg would say or do next.

"Wait. Let me handle it." I entered the room. Both of the men had puffed out their chests and bruiser's right hand twitched near his side. I wondered whether he was packing. What did they think? That I was Meg's pimp? For some reason, Ethan's comment, "Don't pimp out Miranda," played in my head and I had to smother a laugh with my palm.

Meg smiled victoriously. I wanted to smash her face in.

I studied the trio, realizing I had absolutely no idea what to say to spring Meg.

"They're threatening to call the cops," said Meg.

I nodded, weighing that option. Would that help Meg in the long run? Rehab obviously hadn't. Jail, though? Did that help anyone?

"I'm sure you'd rather not draw more attention to the matter," said the sleazy manager.

That settled it for me. "Of course not," I said.

"She's not allowed back here. Ever." The manager glared at me as if I had control over Meg.

I nodded. Let him think I did. The last thing I needed was more Meg drama. Fucking hell, if this got out at school … And Sarah stood right outside the door. The only person who truly loved me and Meg threatened that.

Meg, probably realizing she had one chance to get out of this mess, hid behind me. I shook the manager's hand. "Thank you."

When Meg and I exited the room, Sarah jumped to attention and I motioned with a palm for her to wait. Meg took the opportunity to slip her arm through mine. I groaned.

Outside, I asked the doorman for a cab.

"Fort Collins," I told the driver when the cab appeared, shoving Meg into the back seat.

"What? That's halfway to Cheyenne. No way." The driver motioned for Meg to get out.

"How much?"

He must have sensed my desperation. "Three hundred."

"Done." I tossed the cash onto the passenger seat. Fortunately, I had stockpiled some dough for the weekend.

"Lizzie — " Meg started, but I sighed to silence her.

"Not now. I'll call you."

The driver slammed on the gas, and I watched the vehicle slip around the corner.

"Jesus fucking Christ," I muttered.

Now what? I needed a moment before dealing with Sarah. I

sat on a bench and leaned my head against the wall.

"Women," the doorman said, probably hoping to ease the awkwardness.

It didn't work. Fortunately, a limo pulled up and he left to attend to the couple and their baggage.

Five minutes later, Sarah appeared, tugging the suitcase I'd purchased yesterday for our romantic weekend behind her.

Our first ... and probably last ... weekend away together, I thought.

Chapter Seventeen

SARAH SAT ON THE BENCH next to me.

Neither of us moved to speak. My mind was flipping through one explanation after another, but when it came down to it, each and every one was useless. *Just tell her the truth. Tell her everything about Meg*, my brain said.

But the truth was too humiliating.

How could I admit to everything Meg had put me through? I kept hearing Sarah's comments about Haley. How she didn't understand how Haley could let someone treat her that way. Did she have no shame?

"We need to talk," Sarah said eventually.

I nodded.

She glanced toward the front door. "Not here, though. I'm sure the manager will be out soon to make sure we've left."

I cracked a weak smile. "I've definitely made an impression on him."

"He's not the one you should be concerned about." Her tone was sharp as

she stood and reached for the bag.

"Here, let me." I lugged it to my car. Sarah climbed into the passenger side.

Before I even started the engine, she said, "You remember that night I surprised you after the opera. You made a comment about ladies of the night ..." Her accusation hung in the air.

"And?"

"I thought you were kidding."

"I was!" I stared at her, shocked. "Sarah, I have never paid for sex. The thought hasn't even crossed my mind. Never."

"Yet you employ Miranda, who moonlights as a hooker."

"How was I supposed to know that? It's not like she listed it on her resume." I threw my hands up in the air, already feeling guilty about the lie.

"You have to fire her."

"I can't fire Miranda!" The entire situation was getting out of control, and at warp speed. I covered my face with my palms.

"Give her enough money and ..."

I peeked through my hands. Indecision furrowed Sarah's brow. "God, do you really think she's suicidal? I keep thinking about my student and then about Miranda. The desperation in her tone when she said how she can't go on." Sarah rubbed her eyes.

Was this my way out of not firing Miranda? I'd never find another person who could make every surface in the bathroom sparkle. But maybe I *had* to fire her now, because if Sarah ever laid eyes on the real, dependable dowdy old Miranda ... That didn't bear thinking about either. God, what a mess!

"Listen. M-Miranda obviously has issues. I knew her from school. She hit a rocky patch and started cleaning to make ends meet. I wanted to help. I didn't know about all the ways she tried to make ends meet. Not until today, I swear, Sarah. But I'm not sure I can fire her. Maybe I can help her instead of — "

"Help her? How?" Sarah said, but her tone was soft rather than confrontational. "Send her to therapy? Pay off her bills? Buy her a place?"

Shit. Did Sarah expect me to foot the bill for all that for Meg? "Uh …"

"What?" She spun on me, alarm back in her voice. "We have to help her, Lizzie."

"I … she's just my maid … I mean, we were in school together, but how involved do I really need to get?" The words slipped out as if the situation were true and my cleaner really was prostituting herself.

"How would you feel if Miranda actually killed herself?" Sarah's eyes started to brim with tears. "And you had done nothing?"

Was she seriously getting this worked up about a woman she thought she'd never even meet until today? *Jesus, Lizzie! She hasn't met Miranda. Focus!*

"Let me talk to her."

"I want to be there," she said.

Oh, my God! I wanted to slam my face into the steering wheel. How had I moved beyond clueless to goddamned stupid so quickly?

"I don't think that's a good idea," I said. "I'm sure she's embarrassed by … everything. I want her to be able to open up to me." I took Sarah's hand and squeezed it. "I'll take care of Miranda. I promise." And by that, I meant I'd take care of Meg. Once and for all. It was time to get Meg out of my life completely.

AFTER A TENSE, quiet drive back to Fort Collins, Sarah wasn't in the mood to come back to my place, and I was hesitant to drop her off in Loveland alone.

"Is there anything you'd like to do?" I asked as we approached the highway exit. "I'd hate to end the weekend on this note."

She laughed. "You mean finding out that Miranda is turning

tricks." She sighed. "It was such a lovely weekend until then."

"It's still early. We can salvage the rest of today," I said, feeling relief rush back into my chest. "You name it and we'll do it."

"Let's see a movie."

I bottled up a groan. "Oh, do you know another movie featuring talking stuffed animals?" I joked, hoping to further ease the strain.

"*The Beaver*."

"You've got to be joking."

"Nope. Technically, it's not a stuffed animal but a hand puppet."

"Sounds great. I'm in." I reached across and squeezed her thigh.

"I don't think it's playing anymore. Besides I'm not sure I would like *The Beaver*," she said in all seriousness. Her phone beeped with a text message, and she pulled out her cell and checked it in eerie silence. After a minute or two, she said, "Ah, I just googled it. I know what we'll see."

"Are you going to fill me in?"

"Nope. Trust me, you'll love it."

"WHAT'D YOU THINK of the movie, Lizzie?"

"I liked it more than I thought I would."

We were snuggled up in Sarah's bed. I wasn't a fan of her place, but I'd be a fool to press my luck today, of all days.

She'd taken me to see *The Artist*, a movie I'd heard others rave about.

"Much better than the last one," I added.

"I thought you'd love it."

I toyed with her nipple. "Really?" We hadn't had sex earlier, but Sarah favored sleeping naked, and I preferred her to.

"Considering all the black-and-white movies you own, it seemed like a sure thing."

I realized she was much more observant than I gave her credit for, and it made a twinge of worry constrict my brain. I needed to fix the Meg/Miranda disaster – pronto.

"You scared?" Sarah's smile confounded me.

"Scared? What do you mean?" Was I frowning? Had she realized I was thinking about what happened earlier?

"I don't think you're used to people paying attention to you," she said. "You're finding it unnerving."

"Oh, please. I'm a lecturer. I'm used to being the center of attention."

"Not in your personal life you aren't. When's the last time you had someone over to your apartment? Not counting your hooker, of course."

"My hooker!"

"Well, I certainly didn't hire her."

It was a relief that Sarah was injecting some humor into the situation.

"Am I right?" She pushed.

I shrugged.

Her bare breasts rose and fell as she laughed. "That's what I thought."

"Whatever." The conversation was making me nervous. I focused on her nipple again as a distraction.

The buzz of her phone interrupted us, and she glanced at the screen and sighed.

"You need to get that?"

"Nah."

I was curious about who was calling, but I didn't want to seem overly inquisitive, so I let it slide. During the movie, sitting with my hand on her thigh, I'd noticed her phone vibrate several times, alerting her to missed calls or texts. Occasionally, I'd spied her clandestinely checking them with a pained expression on her face. It had to be Haley.

"You sure you don't want to take the call?"

She cupped my chin with her palm. "This is what I want to do." Her lips met mine.

I wasn't going to argue.

"Besides the drama earlier, it was a wonderful weekend." Sarah's eyes glistened, and I felt an immediate urge to alleviate her sadness. "Thank you. I really needed to get away for a couple of days."

I nodded, understanding. It felt good to leave my books behind, to relax and do things that had absolutely nothing to do with my PhD program. "We should do it more often – minus Miranda."

"Yes. And now that we don't have to hide our trust funds, it'll be easier to get away."

"What a relief. I felt horrible when Ethan told me the sweater-vest you bought me was cashmere. I almost gave it back."

Sarah biffed the back of my head. "You can't give back a gift!"

I rubbed my head, grinning. "I know. Ethan told me. And then I toyed with the idea of renting a car for you, since I thought you couldn't afford to get a new one." I tickled her side.

She laughed and squirmed, all tension drained from her body.

"God you're beautiful, Sarah," I murmured.

She enveloped me in her arms. "Say it again."

"Say what?"

Sarah bit my lower lip, tugged at it with her teeth. "You know what."

"That you're beautiful?"

"Yes. That."

"You are absolutely beautiful. And your body ..." I traced a hand down her side. "Let me show you how stunning I think you are."

Her neck felt warm beneath my lips. She let out a small moan and said, "I love the way you make me feel."

I grazed her nipple, and her sharp intake of breath was all the motivation my tongue needed to work its way down her stomach. "I need to taste you."

Her hips responded, guiding the way, the wetness between her legs gleaming like a lighthouse, navigating the ship of my kiss to safety.

I found my way.

Chapter Eighteen

"BEFORE WE FINISH TONIGHT, I want to invite all of you to Mrs. Marcel's annual end of the year barbecue," Dr. Marcel said, handing out the handwritten party invites.

Each May, the Marcels had all the grad students over to celebrate surviving another grueling year.

Mrs. Marcel's loopy handwriting was even shakier than last year. Janice nudged my leg with her toe. "Gosh, you never pay attention when it comes to this stuff."

I glanced up. "What? I'm sorry."

Janice jerked her head to Dr. Marcel.

"As I was saying, since it's only the three of you this year, I think it would be nice if you each invited a guest. The more the merrier!"

"I have a date, and I'm sure Janice will bring her steady," William said.

Janice and I exchanged a glance over his word choice. Steady? Was that East Coast code for significant other?

William frowned at us and continued, "But, Lizzie ... no chance." His lips contorted into an evil sneer.

Janice must have kicked him under the table because his knee suddenly whacked the bottom of the seminar desk.

Since it's just the three of us, I thought, *Janice and William are bound to act even more like siblings.* I couldn't think of a single seminar when Janice hadn't kicked William at least once over the last year.

"Ouch! It's no secret Lizzie is completely opposed to relationships." William hissed, leaning down to rub his shin.

"What makes you think that?" I instantly regretted asking. Why did I care what William thought? Why had I voluntarily just entered the Meg danger zone?

"I don't think we need to go into that. Let's just say, you suck at them."

"She does not!" Janice jumped to my defense.

Dr. Marcel watched us as if we were his grandchildren fighting over who would get to eat the ears off a chocolate Easter Bunny.

"Really?" William whipped his head around to meet Janice's glare. "The one with Meg ended in disaster."

"You can't blame Lizzie for Meg's behavior." Janice placed both palms on the table and leaned forward. "You have no idea what went on in that relationship. It's time you let it go, Willy Boy."

"I have no idea! I know when they broke up Meg quit the program. Before that, she'd been the star pupil." He swung around to confront me. "And Lizzie couldn't handle that because she thinks she's better than the rest of us."

Although he was speaking directly to me, he'd referred to me in the third person. It was hard not to laugh right in his face.

"Careful, William. I think your insecurities are shining through again," said Janice.

Dr. Marcel seemed to be watching Janice and William as if they were putting on a play. His eyes shone with intrigue, but his body language was nonexistent. I'd often wondered if he just tuned us out when we squabbled.

William sucked in his cheeks to the point I thought he might swallow them completely.

It was time to enter the fray again. I cleared my throat and uttered, "I have a date."

"What?" Janice and William asked simultaneously. William's brow knitted itself into a perplexed knot.

I returned Janice's smile and then turned to my professor. "Is there anything I can do to help with the party?"

Dr. Marcel waved a hand. "Mrs. Marcel would have my head on a platter if I asked grad students to bring anything. She's under the impression all you three do is teach and study." He winked at me.

On my way out, Dr. Marcel motioned for me to join him in his office.

Dutifully, I followed. I fidgeted in the leather chair, unsure what he wanted to discuss.

"I thought I'd tell you that Meg stopped by."

I bit my lower lip, nodding absently.

"She wants to come back." He folded his hands on top of his desk.

"Meg's a brilliant student," I managed to say.

"That she is," he replied. "Her actions, though, are hard to ignore." He tapped his thumbs together. "Do you have any insight or advice about what I should do? Let her back or give a recommendation, maybe?" His kind eyes bored into mine as if he was demanding evidence, evidence that no one else knew.

Flummoxed, I swallowed. How could I confess all? It was nice that he was treating me as an equal, but how could I admit the whole truth and nothing but the truth? And what would he think of me if I did?

Perhaps realizing what a bind he'd put me in, Dr. Marcel

waved one hand. "I'm sorry, Lizzie. You're right. It's a decision I should make. I shouldn't put any pressure on you to say anything."

He didn't show any sign that he was willing to push me on the topic, but I was certain he was hinting that no matter what I said, he wouldn't judge me. But he didn't know everything, so how could he make such a promise?

We stared at each other, not sure where to take the conversation.

"Who's your date?" he asked, putting that unpleasant business behind us.

"Do you remember Sarah Cavanaugh, the high school English teacher you introduced me to last semester?"

A broad smile spread over his face. "Ah, such an enthusiastic, lovely young woman. Good for you." He shuffled some papers on his desk, which I took as a sign I should skedaddle. I stood.

"Safe ride home," he said as I waved good-bye.

In the stairwell, I fell against the wall. How was it possible that Meg was now haunting every aspect of my life?

"WHAT ARE YOU doing on the twenty-first?" I asked Sarah. "It's a Thursday."

"Can't think of a thing besides schoolwork. Got a better offer?" Sarah took a slow lick of her gooey, chocolate-chip cookie-dough ice cream.

I'd returned from campus to find Sarah looking adorable in a short skirt and tank top and insisting that we go for a walk. While strolling through Old Town, we'd discovered a new ice cream shop and had taken a seat on a bench outside to eat our desserts.

I licked the trail of mint chocolate-chip that seeped out the bottom of my waffle cone. "Do you remember Dr. Marcel?"

She nodded, enthralled in watching twin boys, no older than five I guessed, who were attempting to walk a golden retriever puppy. The trio would only get a few feet before the puppy entangled one of the boys, or sometimes both, in its leash. It barked happily, and the boys screeched in delight.

"He and his wife throw a barbeque for the survivors of each school year," I continued. "The first year, there were ten of us. Now there are only three."

"Three?"

"Yep. Soon to be only one."

Sarah's gaze turned on me, and her eyes shimmered with worry.

"William is heading back East to finish his dissertation. He got a research internship in Boston. Janice is finally throwing in the towel and marrying Collin to please her parents," I explained.

"That's awful."

I laughed. "Not really. I'm pretty sure she loves Collin. It's just the whole giving-a-woman-away-to-a-man thing that ruffles her feminist feathers. She told me her father made her an offer she couldn't refuse."

Sarah's eyebrows almost met in the middle as she frowned.

"He'll hire Collin to work in his construction firm, buy them a house outright, and pay off both their student loans."

"Will she finish her PhD?"

"I don't know. Her heart was never in it. That was obvious to all, including her parents, I think. For her, it was a way to escape. But who knows? Maybe when she's had some time away, she'll feel like finishing her dissertation. Stranger things have happened."

"You're sure she loves him?"

I bumped Sarah's arm. "They've been together since their

undergrad days. You'll get to meet them firsthand at the barbecue, if you want."

"You're inviting me?" Her eyes crinkled up with shock.

"Yes. If you want to go. It's nothing exciting. You might even be bored to tears. Once the liquor starts to flow, we start debating history, and not just World War II. Last year, we had an hour-long *discussion* about the War of 1812." I made air quotes around the word discussion and sucked another smear of ice cream off my knuckles.

"The War of 1812?"

"Yes. It's quite fascinating actually. To this day, it's hard to determine who actually won, if anyone won at all. The Brits hardly batted an eye at the skirmish. But the Canadians and Americans trumpeted their horns about their resounding victories."

"That does sound fascinating." Her tone implied the opposite.

"Hey, you don't have to go."

"No, I'll go. You said there'll be booze."

"Truckloads. Do you like potato salad?"

She nodded enthusiastically, too busy finishing her ice cream before it melted to give a verbal response.

"Good. I've been told Mrs. Marcel makes the best potato salad."

"You haven't tried it?" Ice cream dribbled down her chin as she spoke, and she wiped it with a half-disintegrated napkin.

"Not a fan, but it's her specialty."

"Lizzie! You have to at least try some. Sometimes I'm shocked by how truly clueless you are when it comes to social situations. Yuck!"

I was fairly certain the *yuck* referred to the river of goo cascading down her hand, not my social ineptitude.

I handed her my napkin. "Odd that it's so warm today. Just

last week I was still in my winter coat. Of course, knowing Colorado weather, it may snow next week."

Sarah cleaned up to the best of her ability before attacking her cone with gusto, determined to finish it once and for all. Afterward, she ran back inside to wash her hands. When she came outside again, she plopped down next to me on the bench and said, "This year you *are* sampling the potato salad."

Not much got her off track once her mind was set.

I sighed. "How much do I have to eat?"

"One spoonful — just so you can compliment her on it."

I bit my lower lip, feeling like a child who had refused to eat veggies. "All right. Just for you." I leaned over and kissed her cheek.

"Not for me. For Mrs. Marcel."

"Ugh. Don't put that image in my head. Here I was trying to imagine licking ice cream off your body, and you mention Mrs. Marcel."

Sarah whipped around to face me. "You were?"

"Yes. I was. Not now, though."

"How can I get you back in the mood?" She stroked a finger seductively down my bare arm.

"That's working."

She blew a few loose strands of hair off my neck. Her breath was warm and cookie-scented. Standing, I tossed the rest of my cone into the trashcan and reached out to help her up. "Home. Now."

"Yes, ma'am!" She saluted, then marched in front of me and glanced back over her shoulder. "I like this side of you."

I said nothing, just playfully slapped her butt.

Chapter Nineteen

DR. MARCEL AND HIS WIFE greeted us at the door.

"Lizzie, it's so nice to see you again." Mrs. Marcel hugged me. "And you must be Sarah. Lovely to meet you." She gave Sarah a friendly hug. "Come in, come in." She ushered us into the front room.

Janice and her fiancé, a squirrely-looking man with a goofy grin, stood to shake our hands.

"Hi, I'm Collin," he clasped Sarah's hand warmly and then turned to me. "Lizzie, congrats on surviving another year." His heartfelt handshake enforced his words.

"Thanks. I'm amazed how quickly this year flew by."

A commotion at the front door interrupted, and I heard William's booming voice. I reached for Sarah's hand and gave it a squeeze, noticing a momentary flash of reluctance on her face.

William and his date stood off to the side, and their awkwardness oozed into everyone's body language. Opposed to Collin, William's date made zero effort to fit in, and the two resembled cast-off royalty sent to far-flung territories to interact with the subjects.

"Now that we are all here, let's move out back," Mrs. Marcel suggested, probably in hopes of alleviating the tension. In years past, William and I did our best to rein in our competitiveness for our hosts' sake, but there was always a ripple of unease whenever we were together.

The end of the year barbecues had become such a tradition that it was hard to believe it would be my last with Janice and William. I wouldn't miss William, of course, but it would be hard to say good-bye to Janice. She was like the big sister I never had.

Along the rear of the large backyard was a rock retaining wall that blocked off Mrs. Marcel's garden, which Janice and I helped with every spring. Gardening wasn't my thing, but the Marcels had been so nice to me over the years that I didn't mind getting dirt under my nails a few days a year. In the other corner huddled five aspen trees.

"Help yourself everyone." Dr. Marcel was manning the grill, but he pointed to a large cooler filled with ice, pop, and beer. Next to the cooler, a folding table offered several wine bottles and another folding table held plates, silverware, and napkins. From experience, I knew that within a matter of minutes it would also be piled with heaped platters of food.

I popped the top of a Mountain Dew, and Sarah laughed.

"What? I haven't had one in years," I said.

"You're going to be bouncing off the walls tonight." She selected an Easy Street Wheat, a local beer.

"Is that a bad thing?" I whispered in her ear.

She squeezed my arm. "It depends. Will you be able to stay focused?"

"Stay focused on what?" interrupted Janice.

"Uh ..." My face felt as red as the wine in Janice's glass.

"Never mind." Janice sniggered and then rounded to Sarah. "How did you two meet?"

Before she could answer, William and his date joined us.

"Hi, I'm Sarah." She extended her hand.

"Sarah. Right." He nodded as if he were the head of the CIA and she was talking in code. "I'm William, and this is Pru."

Pru shook my hand and then Sarah's. Her fingers were ice-cold, and the handshake was the weakest I'd ever experienced.

"Is that short for Prudence or Prunella?" asked Janice.

"Prunella." She didn't say anything else, but her pursed lips and death grip on William's arm told me she was a blue blood from back East who felt uncomfortable around the heathens of the West.

"Pru is an old family friend." William patted her hand, suggesting they were more than friends. They'd probably been betrothed since birth.

"That's neat," Janice replied, not bothering to make it sound like she meant it. Her gaze flicked to me, and I knew we were on the same page: Pru was just like William. Collin wrapped an arm around her waist, a Coors Light bottle clutched in his other hand.

Sarah watched William and Pru with an amused smirk. I could tell she was already warming to Janice and Collin.

"So, Sarah, how did you two meet?" Janice asked again. "I'd ask Lizzie, but she's the type who only gives information on a need-to-know basis." Janice nudged my arm.

"I introduced them." Dr. Marcel entered our circle, still holding his barbecue tongs. He snapped them in my direction and then Sarah's, clearly thrilled with his matchmaking skills.

Janice twirled to face me. "Really? Do tell."

I almost blurted there wasn't much to tell, but Dr. Marcel seemed so pleased with himself that I let him continue.

"Sarah came to my office in the hope of sitting in on one of my classes with a group of her students," he told them.

Knowing the story, I tuned out, taking the opportunity to compare the two couples. Janice and Collin melded together naturally, with Janice leaning comfortably against her fiancé and sipping her wine. William and Pru were the exact opposite. She clutched his arm so stiffly they reminded me of a painting of an aristocratic couple from yesteryear: overly formal, vacant eyes, and not a lick of warmth between them.

Out of the corner of my eye, I noticed Mrs. Marcel bringing a tray of food from the kitchen, and I let go of Sarah's hand to help out. I had to hand it to Dr. Marcel. He was weaving quite the tale, considering there wasn't much to relate. No wonder his students loved him. He could make watching paint dry sound interesting. To be honest, he had to; some aspects of history were just as tedious.

"Here, Mrs. Marcel, let me help you." I took the heavy platter from her frail hands. It was overloaded with bowls of potato salad, pasta salad, fresh fruit, baked beans, deviled eggs, homemade mac and cheese, coleslaw, and chips. She was a thin, birdlike woman, unlike the plump professor. I'd always wondered if she was a few years older than him. I knew Dr. Marcel was seventy-one, but she seemed closer to her eighties.

"Thank you. You're always such a help." She touched my cheek. "Oh, dear, I forgot the corn bread in the oven." Mrs. Marcel settled her hopeful eyes on me, and I almost laughed.

"Of course. I'll be right back."

When I returned with the piping-hot cornbread, the group was congregated around Mrs. Marcel and the food.

"Can I get anything else for you?" William asked. He glowered at me as if I were a younger sibling trying to outdo him. Then he shoved a handful of potato chips in his mouth and munched loudly. I tried to suppress a smile at the thought that he was pretending they were my bones.

"That would be lovely, dear," Mrs. Marcel answered. "In the fridge, can you bring the platter with the cheese, tomatoes, lettuce, pickles, and other toppings for the burgers?"

"Be back in a jiff." He kissed her cheek before rushing off like he'd been sent to rescue a kitten from a fire.

I turned to catch Janice's eye, intending to mock William, but noticed a look of concern on her face. She rolled her eyes sideways, in Sarah's direction.

My girlfriend was staring off in space, avoiding all eye contact.

I sidled up to her. "You okay?"

"What?" She flinched as if she'd forgotten where she was.

"Lost in la-la land?" I said.

"No. Just thinking." She adjusted her floral skirt, plastered a smile back onto her face, and sidestepped around me to thank Mrs. Marcel on the spread before us.

Dr. Marcel, still finishing his grilling duties, gestured for me to join him for a private chat. William, who'd returned just in time to witness that, gave an annoyed sniff.

"Do you need a hand, sir?" I asked, joining him.

Dr. Marcel set the tongs aside. "No. It's come to my attention that Meg's request to return to school isn't a secret."

I scratched my chin, not sure where this was going.

"I know I told you I was considering it, but I've decided it's best for … everyone … if she doesn't come back." He squeezed my shoulder. "You don't have to worry."

He had no idea how much worry I carried.

"I've talked with former colleagues back East. One who now teaches at Yale has experience … with Meg's issues. She might be welcome there, as long as she cleans up."

"That sounds like an excellent opportunity." I resisted the urge to jump in the air and tap my feet together. "Does she know this?"

"Yes. She arrived in New Haven this morning."

"What about the drinking?" I held my breath.

"My friend is recommending a place in Florida. If Meg completes the program, she'll be able to start as a research assistant this September." He squeezed my shoulder. Had he done all this for Meg or me? Both, probably.

Mrs. Marcel called to her husband, and he smiled and went to her, leaving me in a daze.

"I take it he finally made up his mind." Janice, never very far in moments like this, said from behind me.

Still dumbstruck, I nodded. Had Meg's name come up while I was inside? And if it had, what did Sarah know about her?

Janice jerked her head in Sarah's direction. "I really like her," she whispered. Hooking her arm through mine, she led me back to our dates.

Me too, I thought, watching Sarah. Her color had returned, her cheeks now almost as pink as her shirt. She glanced at me, but edged away a little when I came to stand next to her.

So many thoughts reeled through my head. Hopefully no one pulled up a picture of Meg, Janice, and me, The Three Musketeers, on their phone or something idiotic like that. Janice would never do such a thing after everything, and William hated me enough he'd never keep any likeness of me on his phone. However, he'd always had a thing for Meg.

"Okay, folks. Dinner's ready!" Dr. Marcel scooped the last burger onto a tray filled with brats, burgers, and steaks, and we all made a beeline for the serving area.

I selected two brats, a burger, some fruit, pasta salad, baked beans, and mac and cheese.

Sarah pointed to my plate. "Here, you forgot this." She scooped a portion of potato salad next to my brats.

"Uh, thanks."

William and Janice raised their eyebrows at each other. They'd teased me in the past for never tasting it.

Mrs. Marcel smiled. "Why, Lizzie, are you finally trying my potato salad?" She patted my back. "It's my grandmother's recipe," she told Sarah. "I still remember the day she taught my sister and me how to make it, so many years ago." Her eyes misted.

"Lizzie told me it's the best." Sarah ladled a much smaller portion onto her plate.

"Here let me, doll." Collin took Janice's plate from her and started to fill it.

"Thanks. You want another beer?"

He nodded, and Janice fished a Coors out of the icebox and refilled her wineglass.

"Teamwork. That's the secret to a great marriage." Dr. Marcel nodded. "That's how the missus and I have lasted all these years." He pinched her cheek tenderly.

"And learning to tune out the other," Mrs. Marcel added with a bemused glint in her eye.

"What's that, dear?" asked Dr. Marcel without a trace of humor.

Janice and Collin sniggered. William and Pru were too busy picking through the steaks and burgers to notice. William's plate was almost as full as mine, but Pru's held only a steak and some fruit.

Sarah's potato salad sabotage meant that half my plate was covered in it, even though she'd said I only needed to eat a bite. I was in the doghouse, and I knew it. But I couldn't muster up the courage to ask whether the problem this time was Meg or Miranda, or both. Or maybe she got another strange text from Haley and was nervous about the Michael situation. I could only hope.

FOR THE FIRST ten minutes of our drive home, Sarah didn't utter a single word.

"Thanks for coming with me tonight," I said in a weak attempt to break her out of her trance.

She nodded.

"Did you have fun?"

"Yeah. You?"

"I've always liked the Marcels. They're the closest thing I have to family."

"Did you — " Sarah stopped abruptly and stared out the side window instead. "Would you mind dropping me off at my apartment?" she said after a while. "I just remembered I forgot something I need for class tomorrow."

"Sure. Not a problem." I put my hand on her thigh. She didn't pull away, but she didn't rest hers on top like she normally did either.

I pulled into the parking space next to her midnight blue Mercedes. "I'll wait for you," I said.

"That's okay. I'm really tired tonight anyway. Call me tomorrow." She threw open the car door and got out.

I leaned over to say goodnight, but by the time I got the word out, she'd already slammed the door shut.

Chapter Twenty

A KNOCK ON THE DOOR made me look up from my book and glance at my watch. It was well after nine at night, and I hadn't heard from Sarah in twenty-four hours, which was beyond worrisome. My stomach dropped. What if it was Meg? She was supposed to be in New Haven!

"Just a minute," I called.

"Oh, take your time. It's just creepy out here. No worries."

It wasn't Sarah's voice. Not Meg's either.

I opened the door. "Janice?"

"There's a creepy guy in your parking lot."

I peered over the railing to see my neighbor, Carl, standing by his Ford F-150. He was dressed in all black, and if a person didn't know he was a total pushover, he might come across as a serial killer kind of guy.

"What's up?" I asked. It wasn't like Janice to stop by my apartment, especially so late in the evening. Something about the visit still reminded me too much of Meg — too many late night Mayday calls to the only person who'd known the truth. After Meg and I split, I'd deliberately put more distance between Janice and myself. She understood. I think she and I felt the same. Meg had been her best friend in grad school. When Meg left, Janice might have felt abandoned or she might have felt free.

"Where's Sarah?" Janice asked, arms crossed over her chest.

"Uh. Not here. Probably at her apartment." I tried to control my voice. I didn't want to sound concerned that I hadn't heard from her and didn't know her whereabouts. We'd only been together a few months. We weren't married. She didn't have to check in with me.

"When was the last time you heard from her?"

"The night of the barbecue."

Janice nodded crisply. "Right."

"Right, what?"

"You have no idea why she's avoiding you today?" Janice tapped her forehead with an inquisitive finger.

"What are you saying?"

"William said something last night – "

"William's an ass." I cut her off.

"That's an understatement. He's a fuckstick. But you know that, and I know that." She waggled her finger back and forth in a perfect impression of a teacher reprimanding a child in the playground. "But Sarah doesn't."

I rubbed my face with both hands. "What does William have to do with Sarah not being here tonight?"

"I'm trying to save your relationship."

"What do you mean?" She now had my full attention.

"While you were helping Mrs. Marcel, William told Sarah he was surprised she wasn't blonde, since you have a thing for blondes. Then he baited her, saying, 'I hope she doesn't ruin your life as well.' Sarah didn't bite, but William ended with a snide comment about the dangers of dating colleagues."

What William had said made me look like an ass, but at least Meg's name hadn't come up.

"He also asked Dr. Marcel if Meg was coming back."

"How'd he know about that?"

"Oh please. You don't think Meg's been hitting him up for money, too. William's even richer than you."

"He said Meg's name?" Sweat prickled my neck.

"Yes. Why? He even hinted that since you wrecked her life Meg had been forced to … well … to take up jobs that were beneath her, and even 'beneath others too' was his callous little joke."

I waved her off, despite the panic roiling under my calm exterior.

Was Sarah piecing all the clues together? Did she know Meg was Miranda?

"Did Sarah say anything once you left?" Janice plunked herself down on the couch and fiddled with the latest *European History Quarterly*. It was open to an article about Bismarck and the cult of personality in Germany. Janice scanned the article. "Can I borrow this?"

Her sudden change in conversation surprised me. "Sure." I thought she was quitting. Why would she need it?

"Well?"

"Yes, take it." I gestured to the journal. "I finished it this morning."

She swatted her knee with the journal. "Not *this*. Sarah! Did she say anything to you?"

I shook my head. "She was oddly quiet. Then she said she'd forgotten something she needed and instructed me to take her home. I haven't heard from her since." I bowed my head as if confessing to a priest.

"Have you called? Texted?"

I collapsed in a chair next to the couch. "I texted, but …" The reality of the situation was dawning on me.

"You have to talk to her," Janice said.

"And say what?"

"The truth."

"*The truth,*" I repeated.

"Yes. I saw the way you were with her last night. I've never seen you look at anyone like that — not even Meg."

"But ..." But what? I didn't even know what Sarah thought was true anymore.

Janice leaned forward and placed a supportive hand on my knee. "I know you. You aren't good at letting people in. And the last time you did, it blew up in your face. You've been running since." She grasped my knee. "Meg told me about your family, about how they treat you. Maybe you should tell Sarah about how Meg treated you, about why you put up with it for so long."

I tried to stand up, but Janice's firm grip kept me seated.

Meg was the only woman I had introduced to my family. Afterward, I swore I would never let them meet another one of my girlfriends. It wasn't that they were horrible to Meg — they were — it was that they were despicable people who treated everyone poorly, especially me. Seeing the pity in Meg's eyes made me vow never to put myself in that situation again. But then I had. Meg turned out to be more like my mom than I'd cared to admit.

"It's no surprise," Janice went on. "But you can't close yourself off from people. It's Friday night. I'm betting you were holed up in your dining room slash office working." She stared at me knowingly.

I didn't bother to refute that since she was spot-on. "And you? What plans did you have this evening?"

"I was having dinner with Collin at Coop's when I saw Sarah with another woman, and Sarah was crying."

I bolted out of my chair. "Crying? I need to talk to her. How long ago was this?"

"I came right over."

I extracted my car keys from my pocket and fled the apartment.

"Wait for me," Janice shouted, running after me.

It was a quarter to ten when we arrived at Coopersmith's. The lights in the dining section were dimmed and tiny candles flickered on all the tables. Janice didn't have to point out Sarah. My eyes instantly sought her out in the crowd. She rested her palm against her face and slumped like she'd just received a punch to the gut.

Janice placed a supportive hand on my shoulder as we approached the table.

"Sarah," I said softly.

Accusatory eyes darted up to mine. Janice must have been prepared for such a reaction; her stiff hand on my back prevented me from stepping back.

"Please. Can we talk?" My gaze flickered from Sarah to her companion, who I assumed was Haley, and back again. I'd never met Sarah's best friend before, but from the fiery expression on Haley's face, she thought I was ten times worse than Hitler.

"I'm Janice." She stuck her hand out to Haley. "Can I buy you a drink at the bar?" She jerked her head in that direction.

Haley refused her hand. "I'm not a lesbian."

Janice let out a tinny laugh. "Right. I like a woman who says what she's thinking. Still, can I buy you a drink?"

Haley sunk deeper into her seat, shaking her head.

"It's okay, Haley. I'll be fine," Sarah muttered in a tone I'd never heard before. She didn't sound pissed, only devastated.

Begrudgingly, Haley stood and snatched her purse from the booth like she thought I might be going to rob her after I pulverized her best friend's heart. Janice threw me an encouraging smile and followed Haley to the bar.

"Can I sit?" I motioned to the seat Haley had just vacated.

Sarah eyeballed me, not speaking for several seconds. Finally, she nodded.

Carefully, I slid into the viper's den.

"Why are you here, Lizzie?"

I guess I would be wondering that as well, if I were her. What should I say? Janice told me you were crying? What if she'd been crying about something that didn't involve me? From the heat coming from her side of the table, I was 99.87 percent sure her ire was directed at me.

"Janice told me she saw you here ... and that you seemed upset." I chewed on my lower lip. *Jesus, Lizzie. You watched all those rom-coms with Sarah. Think of a sappy line.*

"And that concerns you how?"

I put my hand on hers, but she pulled away.

"Sarah."

Her nostrils flared as if daring me to continue.

"Why haven't you returned my texts?" was all I could think to say.

"Been busy." Her crossed arms implied I had to work harder.

God, Lizzie, think! I mentally smacked my forehead. I should have been apologizing or begging for forgiveness.

"I think — "

"I'm really not sure you do." She bit down on her lip with such force I worried she'd sever it.

I rubbed my face with both hands so hard that my fingers pushed against my nose and blocked my passageways momentarily. "William. He's an ass."

"From what I'm learning, you aren't much better."

I stifled a snort. "But what he said — "

"What did he say?" she cut me off.

"He said I ruined a colleague's career. But he's wrong. So very wrong."

"Not just her career. Her life."

"It wasn't my fault. You have no idea what really happened."

"I'm not hearing an explanation."

"Okay. I know you're frustrated with me right now, and from the glower in your eyes, you want to shove bamboo under my fingernails." I paused to see how that would affect her. Her glare didn't soften at all. This wasn't going to be easy. "It's just not easy for me to talk about …"

"Easy for you. What about Meg? Or should I say Miranda?" Sarah slid her phone across the table and I saw a photo of Meg, Janice, William, and me, all smiles at the Marcel's barbeque in my first year of the program. Sarah must have gone home last night and scoured the university's history website for information. Damn the Internet.

She snatched the phone back, fiddled with it and then placed it in front of me. I studied Miranda's website page, which had a photo of my cleaner clear as day and who looked nothing like Meg.

Sarah scowled in anticipation of my response.

I let out a puff of air. "Okay, I know this looks bad. It's true I dated one of my colleagues. It didn't end well. Actually, it was horrendous — "

"Yeah, it's been horrendous for you. Poor Lizzie. Jesus, we ran into your ex at the hotel and you lied and told me she was Miranda. How can I believe anything you say anymore? She also said you'd given her hundreds of dollars. Have you been sleeping with her? Have you been paying her for sex?"

This again? What? No! I shook my head.

"So, she was lying? I know you hadn't dated anyone for over a year. I'd often wondered how you got your rocks off — "

"Oh my God. I didn't pay her for sex, and I didn't have sex with anyone until you." Was I seriously bragging about this?

Could the people in the surrounding booths hear?

"At the moment, I'm more inclined to believe Meg."

"How can you even say that?" I pulled away as if she'd struck me.

Sarah's huff of frustration reminded me she didn't know everything.

"Sarah, I ... I ..." God, she'd think I was as pathetic as Haley. Could I do this? Could I tell her? Would that convince her to give me another chance? After all, we'd already established the truth wasn't exactly my forte. Then it came to me — the perfect smokescreen. "Me? I'm the liar? You lied about your car and about your trust fund. And then there's Haley."

"What about Haley?"

"You disappeared for a whole week and stayed at her place. And all the text messages. For weeks I thought I was the other woman."

"So now *I'm* a liar and a cheat. Great. Thanks, Lizzie. Why were you with me?"

"Because I fell in love." It was the truth, at last.

Sarah sniffed. "Do you even know what the word means?"

"I know I don't want to spend the rest of my life without it. And I know you're the one person who makes me happy."

"This is happy?" Sarah spread her arms wide apart and gestured to the two of us. "Right now I'm so furious with you I could throttle you. How you can sit there and compare my *omissions*" — she emphasized the word, eyes narrowed — "to your outright lies over the Meg and Miranda situation is ... is ... I can't think of the word to describe someone cocky enough to pull that crap."

"Attitudinizer."

She scowled at me. "I wasn't asking for a word! But maybe another one that starts with A is more appropriate."

Did she just call me an asshole? Not that I could blame her at the moment.

"I'm sorry," I said, but I still couldn't come out with the truth about Meg. Maybe Sarah was right: maybe I was an asshole, a fuckstick even. It was easier to let her think that and not the truth. She'd made it clear that she loved Haley, but she didn't respect Haley. Not completely. Not for letting Michael treat her the way he did. And Meg. Not only did Meg abuse me, but she had been blackmailing me for over a year. Was there a way to win Sarah back without spilling my guts? "Look, I'm not trying to pretend anything," I continued, my voice catching. "I'm just saying we both kept things under wraps."

A malicious grin appeared on Sarah's face and her dark bob bounced around as she shook her head. "All along I thought you were clueless. You aren't clueless, Lizzie. You're just a fucking manipulator."

The word slashed through me far more than the word *asshole* had. Meg had manipulated me for months. To have Sarah feel the same about me — it was too much.

I reached across the table for her hand. "Sarah, please — "

"You are a piece of work." She spat the words and then stood. "I've had enough," she hissed as she left the table.

I watched helplessly as she marched over to Haley and yanked on her friend's arm. Both of them hotfooted it toward the door, Haley looking back with an expression that warned me I should watch my back. Janice just stared at me open-mouthed and then raised both hands in the air as if to say, *What gives?*

I gawked back, throwing my own hands up in the universal I-don't-know gesture. Around us, several people watched, amused.

I sighed.

"Fuck it," I muttered. Springing to my feet, I immediately chased after her.

Outside, Sarah was nowhere to be seen. I scanned the sidewalk, left and then right, hoping for a clue. Rom-coms told me to look for a scarf on the ground. That's how it always happened in the movies.

Janice rushed up behind me. "Which way?"

"You go right. I'll go left." I didn't wait to explain what she was supposed to do if she found them.

It didn't take me long to realize they hadn't gone in my direction at all. Shit!

I wheeled around abruptly, nearly knocking over a woman in her fifties. Her husband clutched my arm and shoved me aside. "Watch it!"

"Sorry," I shouted over my shoulder as I ran.

Not even fifty yards away, I saw Janice talking to Sarah by the fountain in the middle of Old Town. Hands clasped, Janice resembled an eager defense attorney pleading for the jury not to convict. From my vantage point, I noticed Sarah's squared shoulders softening. Both of them turned when they heard me approach. Haley huffed in revulsion.

"Sarah, please. Hear me out."

Chapter Twenty-One

"NO," SARAH SAID, BUT HER eyes were sympathetic, which confused the hell out of me.

"No?" I staggered back a step.

"I want to speak to Janice."

"Janice?" both Haley and I asked at the same time.

Janice put her arm around my shoulder. "It's okay. Let me talk to her," she whispered, walking me a few steps from the group.

"Lizzie," Sarah called out, and I spun hopefully. "Can you please drive Haley home?"

"Yeah, sure," I replied, eyes downcast so she couldn't see my disappointment.

"What? No. I'm not riding with *her*." Haley backed away as if I were Josef Mengele.

"Haley, please. I need to talk to Janice alone," Sarah said.

I wanted to shout, "What the fuck?" but I remained mute. Sarah's body language indicated she was yielding, and I didn't want to jinx anything.

Haley's eyes were imploring her, but Sarah smiled wanly and gave her friend a hug. "Please do this for me," I heard her say.

I motioned for Haley to follow. My car was two blocks from

the town square, and I was dreading every moment I had to spend with this girl who obviously hated my guts.

In the car, I wondered how Sarah could be such good friends with someone so morose. Haley clutched her purse in her lap, holding it against her like body armor. Not once did she look at me or speak, except to tell me where she lived. If not for her demeanor, she'd be gorgeous. I wondered what she was like on a good day. Not that I was curious to find out.

Fifteen minutes later, I pulled in front of Haley's building and she leaped out before the car came to a complete stop, slamming my car door with such force that I swear the steering wheel shook.

"No need to say thanks," I grumbled through clenched teeth. I waited for her to enter her apartment, not wanting to have to explain it to Sarah if something happened to her. When she was secure inside, and out of my sight, I let out a long, tired breath.

My phone vibrated: a text from Sarah.

Meet me at IHOP in an hour.

IHOP? That wasn't Sarah's normal type of place. Given the hour, though, it made sense that was where Sarah and Janice decided to chat. Most eateries, besides bars, were closing. Plus, her request made it clear she didn't want to be alone with me. *Is this my last meal? Have a pancake and then never see Sarah again?*

Sarah's car was already in the lot when I pulled in. I sat in the parking area of IHOP for forty-five minutes before I ventured inside five minutes early. Janice sat at a table in the back — by herself. My heart plummeted to my feet with such force I was sure it would crash all the way to China. Had Sarah managed to sneak out the back?

She waved me over, perkier than the last time I saw her. Was she putting on a brave face? Was she preparing to say that she'd tried but failed?

I slid into the booth across from her.

"Cheer up, Lizzie. She's willing to talk to you now."

"What did you say to her?"

"The truth. That William has been after you since Dr. Marcel chose you over him. That Meg was self-destructive. I think Sarah's starting to come around."

"Where is she?" I scouted the premises, not seeing her.

"In the bathroom." Janice got up to leave.

"Where you going?"

She tipped her head back and laughed. "Don't panic. You can do this."

"But — "

She put a hand on my shoulder. "Just be yourself … but not completely." She winked, but her shoulder squeeze was supportive.

"Hello." Sarah approached the table tentatively.

"Let's do dinner soon," Janice said, hugging her as if they'd been best friends since elementary school.

Sarah nodded but stepped back. "Thank you."

"No problem," Janice said. "Lizzie is special." She didn't make it sound like a compliment, and Sarah got a chuckle out of that, too.

Sarah slipped into the booth, and I watched Janice march out of the restaurant without looking back. My tongue felt swollen, rendering me incapable of speech. At the last moment, Janice turned and gave me a thumbs-up. It made me crack a smile.

"I like her," Sarah said, gazing at Janice's retreating back.

"Y-yeah," I slurred. My tongue was working again, but my mouth seemed full of sand. "You okay?" I asked, noticing her red, swollen eyes. I reached for her hand. This time, she didn't pull away.

"A little better now. This hasn't been a fun night, though."

She waited for me to say something. Anything.

"I'm sorry. I never wanted to make you feel ..." I couldn't say *manipulated*.

"Are you hungry?" She picked up the laminated menu.

I shook my head.

"Seriously? You aren't hungry?"

"Not really."

She tilted her head, scrutinizing my face. "I don't know what to say. I shouldn't have jumped to conclusions without talking to you."

I snorted. "How could you not — after everything? Meg. William. Miranda. I'm really sorry."

"I'm pretty sure Miranda is the only innocent party in this whole mess." Sarah smiled.

I tried to return it, but found I couldn't. Janice paved the way for me, but she didn't know it all, and I knew I'd finally have to come completely clean for the first time or it would never work with Sarah.

The haggard waitress approached. "Can I get you two anything?" Her tone implied we should order immediately or leave.

"Tea?" I suggested out of fear.

"Coffee for me. And ..." Sarah glanced down at the menu. "Can we get the appetizer sampler to start, please?"

The waitress grunted a yes as she waddled off.

"To start?"

"I eat when I'm upset." Sarah's eyes darted away from mine, and she swiped them with her sleeve.

I felt terrible. "What can I do to make you feel better?"

"Talk to me. Tell me about Meg. All of it."

I nodded, blinking away a tear forming in my right eye. I ignored it, not wanting to let on that I was on the verge of crying.

Sarah didn't ignore it. She reached out and wiped it away with the sleeve of her sweater.

"Meg ..." I started, quickly faltering. I sucked my lower lip into my mouth.

Sarah gave me an encouraging nod.

"I met her when I first started the program. She and Janice were two years ahead of me. I was dazzled by her at first. She was Dr. Marcel's superstar. She could do no wrong. For a long time, I thought she walked on water."

"Until?" Sarah stroked my hand with a finger, encouraging me to continue. "It's okay."

"She wasn't very nice to me." I sat up straighter, placed both hands on my head, and blinked away some tears. "At first she was, but then I got to know the real Meg. The behind-closed-doors Meg. The alcoholic Meg." I closed my eyes tightly.

"The bitch Meg," Sarah said, and I realized she must have finally remembered their first meeting.

"God, she was so fucking mean," I continued. "When she drank, which was often, she was so belittling, blamed me for everything. Janice was good friends with her, but even she didn't know the whole truth at first. Eventually, she saw how Meg treated me. I don't think Janice knew how bad her drinking was until a year or so after Meg and I started dating. Maybe it was my fault."

Sarah gripped my hand. "No, Lizzie. It was not your fault. The only one to blame for Meg's drinking is Meg. Don't ever think it was your fault."

Her forcefulness surprised me and calmed me.

"I know that — knew that," I corrected myself. "At least most of the time. I tried to help her. I really did. I paid for her rehab." I shook my head. "I don't think she wanted my help. Meg was always so stubborn. Everything had to be on her terms. When she crashed and burned out of the program — "

"How?"

"She showed up drunk for a conference Dr. Marcel was hosting. Meg was one of the speakers."

Sarah put a hand on her chest. "Really?"

"Yeah. It was so unlike anything she'd done. Dr. Marcel was devastated. I think he suspected she liked to party, but she'd never let it interfere with school or her research. Never."

"What happened?"

I covered my face with my palm. "The day before, we really got into it. Meg was screaming at me. She got totally out of hand. It wasn't unusual for her to push or shove me. Once she pushed me so hard I lost my balance and I sprained my wrist. When really drunk, she'd corner me to scream in my face. She'd even placed a forearm over my throat …" I covered my mouth and let out a shaky sigh. "It sounds so bad, saying it out loud. But then, I could explain it all away … Make excuses … She didn't mean to hurt me … But the last time … Before I knew what had happened, she'd hit me. Split my lip." I massaged my lip with my fingers, remembering my humiliation. "She didn't stop there. I had bruises …" My voice caught, so I motioned to my arms and chest to finish the thought. "I was supposed to be leaving that night for a different conference back East, so the last thing I said to her was that I was done. I couldn't be with her anymore."

Sarah swallowed visibly, tears welling in her eyes, but she didn't stop me.

"I didn't even know what happened, about her showing up drunk. When I got back from my conference, all her stuff was gone from my apartment. She didn't live with me, but … well, you know … things accumulate over time. And she never had a key, so I still have no idea how she got in. Dr. Marcel broke the news to me that she'd been kicked out of school."

"How long were you two together?"

"Over two years."

"Was it bad the entire time?"

I licked my lips and then rubbed them together, holding everything in. "I ..."

"It's okay." Sarah looked down at the table. "You don't have to explain all at once."

"No, I think I should. I was so desperate to keep her in my life. To feel love ... My family, well I never really felt I belonged there. And then Meg happened, and she wanted to be with me. But she really only wanted to control me, I think because she couldn't control herself. I flipped through that book you got after the Haley/Michael situation. The one about abusive personalities." She nodded. "It made me feel so stupid. I missed so many warning signs." I rubbed the top of my head. "I kept ticking them off: the interrogations when I returned home late. Her forcing social isolation — I was never one to hang with friends much to begin with, but to be told I couldn't ... That was frustrating. She would accuse me of sleeping with everyone, even William. The verbal abuse. The insults. She was a pro at twisting innocent comments into insults. I was constantly afraid to say anything out of fear of instigating an episode. I started to keep track of the episode-free days. Sometimes I could go days without seeing Mr. Hyde. Sometimes Mr. Hyde popped out no matter how hard I tried to behave. I tried so hard not to make her angry." I rubbed my thighs with sweaty palms.

Sarah wiped a tear off her cheek. My eyes brimmed.

"It got to the point where I didn't know which way was up. Janice spent many nights trying to talk some sense into me. I always made excuses for Meg, always explained the abuse away. I didn't want to admit to myself that I was being tormented by my girlfriend. I still don't. Except for that time when she showed up drunk at the conference, Meg appeared perfect to all of our acquaintances. The star grad student everyone wanted to emulate. Even today, William blames me for ruining Meg. For destroying her career. I was terrified to end the relationship because I didn't want all this to come out. Meg threatened on many occasions to tell the truth – *her* truth. I couldn't face it. And then when she beat me" – my voice cracked and I had to recover before continuing – "that changed me. It scared the crap out of me, and the mortification ..." I covered my eyes.

Sarah sniffled.

The waitress arrived with our drinks. "I'm sorry it's taking so long for your order. It'll be out as soon as possible." With that she left.

I sighed. Sarah smiled meekly as a way to say please continue.

"Since that day, I promised myself I would never let a woman get to me again, for better or worse. The thought terrifies me. And then I met you." I glanced in her direction. "All thoughts of Meg flew out of my head. And there was only you. But ..."

"But what?"

"I'm still scared."

"Of what? I'd never hit you." She placed a hand over her heart.

"Being hit only hurts for a bit. But not being enough for someone ... that frightens me." I stifled a sob, and Sarah handed me a napkin to dab my eyes.

"Even after you found out about Haley you didn't say anything. Why didn't you trust me?"

"You've been telling me all along I'm clueless, so very clueless. Besides, you may not remember this, but when you told me about Haley you said ..."

Sarah rested her hands on mine. Tears dripped down my cheeks. "I remember, but Lizzie ... if I had known – "

"Then you'd be there for me as a friend like you are for Haley. Not judge, but not understand and secretly question how I could be so weak."

"I'm so sorry. It wouldn't have been like that. I'm here, now. And I'm not going anywhere."

"You don't know it all yet."

Sarah swallowed.

"Since the breakup, Meg's been blackmailing me."

"How in the world?"

"She's threatened to tell Dr. Marcel that I've plagiarized parts of my master's thesis. Or to say I had sex with a student. She's threatened telling William everything — the sex, the abuse. God knows what other devious plans she's concocted now that she's seen you on more than one occasion. I've been living in dread."

"We'll figure out a way to deal with Meg. I promise."

She looked earnest.

"Dr. Marcel is helping," I said.

"Does he know everything?"

"I'm sure he's guessed plenty, but no. I've never told a soul about all of this. Not even Janice."

"Then how is Dr. Marcel helping?"

"He's helping her get into a program in Connecticut. She just has to clean up her act."

"You don't sound so confident."

"She left rehab early last time." I held up my heavy head with two fingers.

"Let's not think about that, just yet. Maybe the hotel situation was her rock bottom. One can only hope."

"Hope," I stuttered. "What about us? How can you respect me after all of this?"

"Oh, Lizzie. You have no idea how strong you actually are. And no matter what, I'll never stop loving you."

I knew we had only brushed the surface of all the things we needed to say to each other, but fatigue swept over me. "Can we go? I'm exhausted." I had to force my eyelids to stay open.

"Of course," Sarah motioned to the waitress for the check.

"I had them wrap it up for you. Sorry about the wait." The waitress set the box down, stared at me and then at Sarah, and gave a supportive nod. I wondered how many times a week she witnessed people at their worst.

Sarah took out her wallet, threw some cash on the table, snatched up the box, and whisked me outside to my car. Taking my keys, she drove us straight to my apartment.

As soon as we stepped inside my apartment, I couldn't fight off my body's desire to sleep. Sarah held me as I drifted off, her warmth beside me in the bed as I slept. She was still beside me when I jolted up in the early hours, clutching at my shirt and trying to steady my breathing.

Sarah stirred. "You okay?"

"Yeah. Just a bad dream."

She lifted the covers. "Come here."

I nestled into her arms.

"Tell me about your nightmare." She stroked my hair.

"It was nothing. Just about Meg." I hid my troubled eyes, burrowing my head into her bare chest.

"I won't let her hurt you again," she promised, kissing the back of my head.

She held me tight, completely unaware I'd just lied to her again.

I'd dreamed that I lost Sarah and was all alone in the world.

Chapter Twenty-Two

SARAH STIRRED A SPOONFUL OF sugar into her coffee. After waking up terrified, I'd fallen sound asleep in her arms and skipped my bike ride. We decided to have breakfast at home before she went shopping with her mom, and I went on my coffee date with Ethan.

"How much does Ethan know?"

I quirked one eyebrow.

"About Meg? The money?" Sarah took a sip, but kept her eyes glued to mine.

I shook my head. "He knew things with Meg were difficult. He has no idea about the money."

Sarah paused, waiting to see whether I would continue. I didn't. I gathered she was weighing her next words carefully. "Why haven't you told anyone the whole truth? What a burden to carry."

I rubbed the back of my left hand with my right. "I'm an independent person, or so I thought. I had to be. Meg took that away from me. It was like she owned me ... and ... and I had to prove to myself I could be independent again. But ..."

"What?" Her voice was soft and compelling.

"I'm scared it might happen again."

Sarah's expression was understanding, compassionate.

"I'm not saying I want to be alone, but I'm scared of being like that again. It's an ongoing battle." I pointed to my head.

"So, what you're saying is that I should be on the lookout for self-sabotage?" She squeezed my hand to show me she was only joking — partially, at least.

I let out a snort of laughter. "Ethan has already warned me, but it might be prudent for you to stay vigilant, too." I suddenly felt a strong desire to tell her the truth about my dream. I forced down some tea to bury that urge deep inside again.

"What do you mean you had to be independent?" Sarah doused her eggs again with pepper, her brows hoisted as she awaited my response.

"I feel like I've been on my own since I can remember. I spent a lot of time hiding from my family." I looked away again, eyes downcast. "Let's just say they weren't the nicest people to be around."

Sarah nodded. "You have a lot in common with Haley."

I grunted. "I think she hates me."

"Don't worry. She's like that with everyone. It takes time for Haley to warm to people. And you aren't the most open person yourself." She forked some omelet rather aggressively.

I wanted to say I couldn't anticipate hanging out with Haley much, but I thought better of it. I'd only just gotten back into Sarah's good graces. It probably wasn't wise to suggest I thought her best friend was a bitch.

"How are you doing?" she asked. "Last night was long for both of us."

I flashed a half-hearted smile. "I'm okay." I reached for her hand. "But the next time I see William, I'm going to give him a piece of my mind. He's such a fuckstick! Never trust a man who doesn't open his mouth when he speaks."

Sarah choked and covered her mouth with her napkin. "Fuckstick! I never thought I'd hear you say that word."

"Janice calls him that, and it suits him perfectly."

"I really like her."

I swallowed a massive bite of toast. "Yeah. I'll miss her."

"I know I just met her, but there's something about her that pulls me in."

"Then maybe it's a good thing she's leaving. Not that she's gay, but I don't want to take any chances." I smiled. "It's weird, though, that I'm the only one left. Even Ethan quit his program once he completed his master's."

"Well, you still have me and Ethan, even if he isn't in school anymore. And I can tell you I'm not leaving." She squeezed my hand back.

I was positive I must have been grinning like a fool.

"That reminds me; give me your keys." She put out her hand, palm up. "I want to get a copy of your apartment key made today."

I blinked and then stared as if the floor beneath me had just disappeared. I managed to say, "Yeah, good idea," without alerting Sarah to the panic rising inside of me. It confused the hell out of me. I didn't want to lose Sarah; in fact, after this morning's dream, I dreaded it. But the thought of her having a key terrified the crapola out of me, too.

"Have you talked with Meg since the incident in the hotel?" Sarah asked.

"Not yet. I'm sure she'll call or text soon to demand more money. Probably for rehab again."

Sarah slammed her coffee cup onto the table. "Oh, hell no!"

"But I thought you wanted me to help her."

"That was before I knew the whole story and thought she was Miranda. I won't let her hurt you or take advantage of you. Not on my watch."

My phone buzzed, and both of us jumped.

"That better not be her," said Sarah.

"Nope. Ethan. He can't make it today. Stomach flu."

"That gives me an idea." Sarah whipped out her phone. "I have the flu as well."

"Do you need me to run to the store for crackers and Sprite?"

Sarah stopped texting and stared at me slack-jawed. "That's what I'm telling Mom. I don't want to leave you alone today."

"So you're lying?" I teased.

"Not really. Maybe just a little. Just saying I feel tired and there's a flu going around school. Mom hates being around anyone who's ill."

"Ah, I see."

"I don't have to send it," she said, her fingers hovering over the keys.

She had me right where she wanted me.

"Please, send it," I said. "I need you."

Chapter Twenty-Three

IT HAD BEEN THREE WEEKS since I confessed all to Sarah, and it had taken me this long to work up the courage to meet Ethan for coffee. I slumped in my chair and said, "I think I'm in trouble."

Ethan placed a concerned hand on mine. "Don't you worry. We'll get through this together. Who's the father?"

"I'm not pregnant!"

Everyone in Starbucks gawped at me, and Ethan howled with laughter. Holding his sides, he managed to say between gasps, "Sarah shooting blanks?"

I leaned over the table. "Oh, you think you're so funny."

He waved one hand in front of his face. "Okay, I'm sorry. What's the problem?"

"Do you know what I did yesterday?"

"Ran a marathon? No — a bikeathon?" He slapped the table. "Cured cancer?"

"What's wrong with you today?" I peered into his coffee cup. "Did you add whiskey?"

He shook his head, all smiles. "It's summertime! No classes until August. I'm a free man."

"Yes, that's my problem. Sarah isn't in school either, so she's decided we need a project to keep busy. She's forcing me to redecorate my apartment. She made me box up all the books I'm not actively reading for research. I'm only allowed one bookcase. Five shelves!" I stabbed the air with a solitary finger. "She's allowed to have flowers in every room, even in the bathroom, but I only get one bookcase."

Ethan drummed his fingers on his chin. "I wasn't aware you decorated your apartment in the first place. At least, you don't seem the type who would."

"That's what she said!"

He closed one eye and inspected my face carefully with the other. "I think you're missing my point. It's nice of her to fix up your place, make it homier. It won't kill you to grow up some."

"B-but ..." I stammered unable to think of a counter-argument.

Ethan took a thoughtful sip of his coffee. "What's really bugging you?"

I yanked on the elastic band that kept my journal shut. "Nothing, really. It's just weird now that she's not in school. We're always together. She's always at my place."

"Your place? Has the U-Haul arrived yet?" He attempted to hide his smile with his cup.

"Nope, just several trips back and forth from her apartment bringing most of her crap over."

"Talk to her. Don't let this fester."

"Talking isn't my strong suit." I knew deep down he was right. Sarah suggested therapy, but I wasn't sure about that. It killed me telling *her* everything. How would I talk to a stranger?

"No, really?" He stretched his legs, and they nearly reached past the next table. "It was bound to happen."

"What?"

"The newness in every relationship wears off. It's hard to maintain that level of excitement."

"It's only been a few months."

"You lesbians move fast. Now you have to decide."

"Decide what?"

"Whether she's really the one you want, or whether it was just the newness that attracted you."

"How do I figure that out?"

He laughed. "Relationships aren't easy. If they were, there'd be no wars, murders, domestic abuse …" He circled his finger in the air.

I ignored him, especially the last bit. "I just need to get through the summer. In the fall, we'll both be busy, and it'll be easier."

"If you say so. In my experience, turning a blind eye to a problem only leads to more problems. But …"

"But what?"

"You're the type who has to find out the hard way. I just hope I get front row seats to what's going to happen."

"What do you think will happen, smarty-pants?"

"No clue. Only time will tell. It's no secret you'd rather run than deal with your issues."

"What issues do I have besides trust and commitment?" The thought of losing Sarah scared me. Yet, the thought of settling down wasn't pleasant either. Why did things have to change so suddenly? I was finally (hopefully) free from Meg. Couldn't we just enjoy our time together without contemplating our futures? I needed baby steps and Sarah wanted to dive in headfirst.

His phone vibrated. After reading the text, he said, "Goodness, they don't have enough coffee in this joint to get us through that conversation."

"Maybe you and Sarah should hang out this summer," I said. "Both of you are so giddy about not being in school. Some of us like school and feel lost without structure and deadlines." My mind tortured me with thoughts when it had too much free time. If it wasn't getting me worked up about Sarah's need to settle down, it plagued me with thoughts of losing her, as if she'd finally realize I wasn't worth the effort. Maybe therapy was needed. Or a diversion.

He picked up his phone. "What's her number?"

I swatted the idea away. "No way. You and Sarah — not going to happen."

"I'll only say good things. I promise." He crinkled his brow. "You might be right. I can't think of anything good to say."

"Whatever. You've been in couple's therapy for over a year now."

He nodded. "And you know what I've learned?"

I motioned for him to tell me, since I knew he would anyway.

"It's best to talk things through and not run."

"That's what you do? Talk?"

Ethan pointed to his chest. "Me? Hell no. All she does is talk. And talk. And talk."

"And you're implying I'm bad at relationships."

"That's TBD, really." Ethan's smirk didn't alleviate the sense of dread forming in my mind.

To be determined. I guess it really was unknown: the future. Sarah and me. Me and Sarah. Nothing was set in stone. It was a relief to a certain degree. A terrifying relief. I've always hated not knowing where something was going.

THAT NIGHT, WE HAD DINNER plans with Janice. Collin had already flown back to San Francisco, and she was leaving the next day.

"So, you all packed?" I asked, placing a napkin in my lap.

She nodded. "Everything is on the truck, all heading home as we speak."

"Are you going to miss Colorado?"

"Some. Not the winters, though. I never got used to the snow."

"I know she won't say it, but Lizzie's going to miss you quite a bit," said Sarah.

Janice giggled. "Lizzie admit that? No way." She pinned me with a frown and then grinned. "I'll miss you as well."

I swallowed.

Sarah placed a hand on my leg, giving it a tender squeeze.

"I will admit I'm sad I never got the chance to sit in on one of your lectures," I said.

Janice flashed me a funny look. "You didn't know?"

"Know what?"

"Why Dr. Marcel asked us to sit in on your class?"

"No."

"It was his way of forcing William out. He already knew I was leaving. After your stellar performance, it was pretty much settled that any teaching positions Dr. Marcel had influence over would be offered to you, not William. Dr. Marcel sat in on William's class before yours. From what I gleaned from eavesdropping, Dr. Marcel pointed him in a different direction." Her eyes crinkled with humor, making it clear she wasn't sorry for eavesdropping yet again.

"That's why William is moving?"

"Yep. Dr. Marcel helped him find a position he'd be more suited to while he wraps up his dissertation."

I sighed. "That man has always had my back."

"He loves you. And he believes in you." Janice patted my hand. "Just like me."

Everything was starting to fall into place. A sense of calm washed over me.

Sarah and Janice plowed on into wedding conversation. For

a woman so against the concept of marriage, Janice had a lot of ideas about her own wedding.

"So, you two are coming?" Janice asked.

Sarah answered for us. "Wouldn't miss it for the world."

"Who knows, it might inspire you, Lizzie." She regarded me curiously.

"Inspire?"

The two of them cracked up. "You never know. You might find your inner romantic sooner rather than later." Janice laughed.

Inner romantic? Marriage equaled romance? The conversation was bounding into dangerous territory. I knew I had to put a damper on the mood, so I brought up a topic I thought would stop Janice cold.

"How does Collin feel about not having kids?" I asked. She'd always said she would never have kids — hated them actually.

Janice flushed three shades of red. Then she grinned from ear to ear.

"You aren't?" gasped Sarah.

She nodded. "Found out last week." Her expression registered happiness with a tinge of fear.

"Found out what?" I looked between the two of them.

Sarah tapped my leg, rolling her eyes. "She's pregnant."

"What? When? How?"

Both Janice and Sarah shook their heads, staring at me wide-eyed.

"Sometimes I really wonder about you," Sarah said. "How did you even survive before me?"

"Oh, she was barely surviving, and not living," offered Janice, a shit-eating grin on her face.

"Oh, whatever." I frowned at both of them until Sarah leaned over and kissed my cheek.

"Don't let this one go," Janice instructed me. "No one else will ever get you like Sarah does."

I knew right then and there that Janice was right.

Sarah understood me, and she still wanted me.

It was a peculiar feeling — one I wasn't used to.

I shifted a little in my seat, Sarah's hand still warm against my thigh. "Trust me, Janice," I said. "I have no intention of ever letting her go."

AUTHOR'S NOTE

Thank you for reading *A Clueless Woman*. If you enjoyed the novel, please consider leaving a review on Goodreads or Amazon. No matter how long or short, I would very much appreciate your feedback.

You can follow me, T.B. Markinson, on Twitter at @50YearProject, on Facebook, or email me at tbmarkinson@gmail.com. I would love to know your thoughts.

ABOUT THE AUTHOR

TB Markinson is an American writer living in England. When she isn't writing, she's traveling the world, watching sports on the telly, visiting pubs, or reading — not necessarily in that order. She has also written *A Woman Lost*, *A Woman Ignored*, *Marionette*, *Confessions from a Coffee Shop*, *Girl Love Happens*, *The Miracle Girl*, and *The Chosen One*. For a full listing of all her published works, please visit her Amazon Page.

Printed by Amazon Italia Logistica S.r.l.
Torrazza Piemonte (TO), Italy